FRAT WARS

ROYAL SCOUNDREL

A FRAT WARS PREQUEL

SAXON JAMES

1

Dash

Rho Kappa Tau is the worst fraternity on campus. They're all rich, all entitled, and ninety percent of them are white guys with generations of being told they're God's gift to the universe.

Archibald Levine the Third is probably the worst of them.

Unfortunately, he's also the hottest of them too. A total snack with all the confidence of knowing the world was made for him.

"Through here," Larry says, sneaking into the back of the campus's swimming center. We heard there's a Kappa

party going down, and while people like us are never on
the invitation lists, we always find our way in.

Like vermin.

While the Kappa brothers might be the worst type of
people, their deep pockets lead to the best parties.

The back hallways echo with our footsteps, and I have
a split second to worry about us having the wrong night
when we pass the locker rooms and the telltale sound of
music up ahead reaches us.

"Just make sure that I don't get drunk and think swimming in the pool sounds like a good idea," Larry says,
hand resting on the door to the pool room.

We tap knuckles. "I've got your back, man."

"Okay. Time to drink all the free booze we can get our
hands on."

He pushes through into the pool room, and the place is
already wild. People everywhere, including making use of
the Olympic-sized swimming pool, a DJ set up on one of
the diving board platforms, flashing disco lights that make
the room seem like it's spinning, and there, on a makeshift
stage, are the Kappa executives.

Legacies at the university. Deepest pockets on
campus. Probably descendants of the Kappa founding
fathers too, but what the fuck would I know? I'm just a
scholarship kid, trying to live my college life to the
fullest, with a hard-on for the asshole smack-bang in the
center of the stage.

Archibald Levine is wearing an open robe, showing

off his washboard abs and sinfully small swimming trunks that leave nothing to the imagination. They're in blue and silver, his house colors, and resting on his head is one of those stupid fucking crowns they wear to all their parties. The Kappa execs. Also known as League of Royals.

I hate how attracted I am to a twat like Levine. He knows he's hot, and he has women hanging off him at every party. He's alone now, but it won't take him long.

It's near impossible to pull my gaze away from the guy and focus back on finding the liquor. I nod hello to people I'm friendly with as I duck through the crowd. I might be invisible to Levine, but thankfully, to the mere mortals on campus, I'm a bit of a catch. Hooking up has never been easier than at college, and I'll take any chance I get to down a few drinks, get sloppy with someone, and then kiss them goodbye the next day, knowing I don't have to worry about their expectations being anything more than one night.

I find a wet bar stocked with bottles of just about every poison you could want. Tequila was my friend last weekend. It's the drink behind the rooftop strip show I put on that I don't exactly regret but probably wouldn't have done if my brain had been online. Given the large body of water behind me, I skip that choice and go for the rum.

No headaches, no vomiting, just a happy high until it makes me pass out early. Which, considering I can't get my brain off Levine, wrapping up the night sooner than later sounds like a fantastic option.

Grudgingly, I have to admit the party was worth sneaking into. Like all of their parties. The music is a good vibe, everyone's dancing, and even though Larry's gone and ditched me, there are no strangers on the dance floor. I dance with anyone who comes my way, rum sliding down my throat easily.

Splashes and squeals come from the water, laughter rising over the thump of the bass taking over my brain. This is what college is all about. This. The fun, the life, you worry about tomorrow when it comes.

There's a break in the crowd, and when my eyes flick open, I have a direct line of sight to Levine. He's doing that bro-dance, one fist in the air, knees bouncing to the bass as he looks out over the crowd below him.

My breath is knocked clean out of my lungs when his eyes catch mine—

—and pass right over me.

Fucker.

Fucking *elitist* fucker.

I throw back the rest of my drink, brain more than a little bubbly now, and turn to the guy grinding against my side. I don't even bother to check him out before I slam my mouth down over his and get this aggressive, frustrated energy out of me.

I don't want to say I have a crush because I don't know anything about Levine other than I'm pretty sure I hate everything about what he represents. My attachment has nothing to do with him as a person and everything to do with sex. Hot, filthy, fantasy sex.

He'd probably be horrified if he knew the things dream him had done to me. If he knew how many times I'd made him come in my mind. The way those high cheekbones stained red. The way his glossy copper curls turned brown when they were damp with sweat. The way I obsessively tasted every inch of his body I could reach.

Urg, my dick is hard as a mallet as I kiss the stranger in front of me. He tries to wrap his arms around me, but I knock them back, grab his jaw, and tilt his head back to kiss him deeper.

This isn't spooning and exchanging names and talking into the morning. This is me needing to get off. To get this overpowering urge for Levine out of my system.

I break my mouth from this guy's but don't go far.

"You wanna suck my dick?"

"Sure."

That's all I need. I take his hand in mine and drag him from the dance floor and toward the exit door closest to us. It's on the opposite side to the one we came in through, but I assume it leads to another hall, and I'm right. There are a few people around, so we keep going past them, my dick trapped and frustrated in my trunks. The first turn into an empty hallway is where I stop.

"Here will do." It's the first time I look at the guy I'm with properly, and under the harsh fluorescent lights, he's stunning. Still, it plain pisses me off that he's not who I want. "Get on your knees."

"Give me a second, geez," he teases, stepping forward to kiss me again as he undoes my shorts. He's a great kisser too, dammit. I hate that I'm only enduring the kiss instead of getting to enjoy it.

Suddenly, the guy steps back. "Ah-Archibald Levine. Uh, hi."

"Leave." The deep, honey tone slides down my spine, and I jerk around, sure I'm hallucinating.

But no. Barely five feet away is the man I can't get out of my mind.

Before I can stop him, the guy I'd been about to hook up with scrambles, only driving my irritation higher.

"Are you kidding me?" Definitely not the first words I ever thought I'd speak to him, but it's bad enough he cockblocks me mentally—now he's doing it for real as well?

"You're the guy from last weekend" is all he says.

I study him for a second. "What are you talking about?"

With a well-practiced smirk, he opens one side of his robe, and I see a T-shirt tucked into the side of his swimming trunks.

My T-shirt.

He pulls it out and tosses it back to me.

"Caught my strip show, huh?"

Levine chuckles, all deep and rich sounding. "I don't think there was a person at the party who missed it."

"I have a good ass. Sue me."

He doesn't answer at first, and it catches my attention. His confident stare slowly trails over me, awakening the hum of possibility in my veins.

Is he … checking me out?

I'm a confident enough guy, but I know I'm not at his level. I have nothing at all for him to be interested in, nothing to offer him, but if that look means what I think it does, I'm not going to miss my chance.

"Why'd you scare my hookup off?" I ask, stepping closer before leaning casually against the wall beside us.

"I wanted to give your shirt back."

"And you couldn't wait to do that until after he'd sucked my dick?"

His tongue slides over his bottom lip. "Do that a lot, do you? Fuck random men?"

"Whenever I can."

"Why?"

I snort because what kind of question is that? "I'm gay, and it's hot. Why shouldn't I?"

He shifts on his feet, and I swear the distance between us shrinks again.

My heart is going wild with expectation. My brain is still struggling to catch up with the fact Archibald Levine the Third is standing right in front of me in all his embroidered silver-and-navy robe, fake gold-crowned glory.

"Aren't you afraid it will be spread around campus? That people will talk about you?"

"I hope they do. All the guys I'm with would have to say is what an excellent fuck I am, and I couldn't think of better advertising than that." Something twitches across his face, and instinct has me adding, "But I know how to be discreet when I need to be."

"You? Discreet?" This time, Levine steps forward on purpose, and some of the confidence in his gaze slips. "You don't remember what you said to me last weekend?"

Last weekend? Hoo boy, tequila did a number on me. "Why don't you remind me?"

"You said …" He swallows, now looking firmly at the wall beside me. "I tried to give your shirt back then, but you, you said …"

"I'm listening."

"That I could either have your shirt or a blow job. My choice."

Jesus Christ. If I wasn't so on edge about scaring him off, I'd laugh. Apparently, tequila also makes me an over-confident douche canoe. He'd clearly chosen to keep the shirt.

But …

I glance down at where the material is clutched in my fist, and then my gaze shoots right back to him.

There's a moment of uncertainty in his eyes—the weirdest mix of blue-green I've ever seen in my life—as we both process what his giving me my shirt back means.

This wasn't him wanting to return it to its owner. He wouldn't have told me the rest if it was.

Archibald Levine the fucking Third wants me to suck his dick.

Blood rushes to my head, but before I can say a thing, his lips are on mine. He presses against me, backing me into the wall, and I struggle to get my footing and kiss him back and stop from goddamn pinching myself to make sure I'm not dreaming again.

He lets out the most feral growl I've ever heard as his tongue licks into my mouth, and I pour all the desperate lust I've been bottling up into the kiss. It's a frenzied mess of tongue and teeth as we both try to be the one in control and the other doesn't let up. He doesn't touch me anywhere else, but my hands can't stop from diving into his perfect curls, knocking the plastic crown to the floor as I try to meld our motherfucking faces together.

I'm finally, finally, going to get this obsession out of my system.

Only when I dip one hand down between us, sliding over his impressive hard-on, Levine jerks back away from me. There's half a hallway between us as he gasps through bite-puffy lips, "I'm drunk!"

"The fuck?"

"I'm drunk. I don't know what I'm doing." His cheeks are that glorious shade of red, but it doesn't get me off like it normally does. Instead, my good mood crashes.

"You're not drunk."

"What the hell would you know?"

"More than you, apparently. We both know what you came here for. If you've changed your mind, fine, but don't act like you didn't know what you were doing."

His glare fades on his handsome face. "No idea what you're talking about."

I sneer. "Tell that to your dick."

A fresh flush races through him, down his neck to his broad chest, as he hurries to close the robe over the front of him. "It's drunk too."

Through my bitterness at the abrupt end, I figure out what's going on here. Levine, despite his obvious curiosity, is closeted. Can't hate a guy for that, but I *can* hate him for scaring my first hookup off because he wanted to play with me.

"Fine, whatever." I roll my eyes. "You're drunk. So drunk you've already forgotten who I am. I don't care."

The disappointment in his gaze is obvious, but I can't fix it for him. It takes a full three seconds before he moves to leave, but I grab him before he can get far.

His whole body tenses, but I only lean in to hiss, "Word of advice: next time you want to *get drunk*, don't chase off a guy's sure thing. It's a fast way to make him hate you."

Levine tugs his arm out of my reach and leaves.

I'm left to watch the hottest ass I've ever seen walk away, dick not even close to waning after that disappointment.

2

Archie

I walk out of the party and don't look back. It's too hot and suffocating in there, not to mention my cock is trying to hulk smash out of my swimming trunks.

I'm already stumbling halfway across campus before I brush my hair back and realize the stupid crown is missing. My brothers are going to kill me, but no way am I going to risk going back for it.

How stupid was I to drop the fucking thing? Next execs meeting, they're all going to know I've lost it, and then half of them will be pissed at me for not taking the royalty thing seriously, and the other half will pepper me with questions about where I lost it and how I didn't realize. None of those are questions I want to go near.

From now on, my life's focus is never, ever seeing that man again.

That man I can still taste on my lips.

What the hell had I been thinking? Sure, witnessing his naked strip show last weekend had been the most sinfully sexy thing I've ever seen, but it didn't mean I had to do anything about it. It definitely didn't mean I had to hold on to his sweaty, ratty T-shirt for an entire week in the hopes I'd run into him again.

The unkempt black hair, his shrewd eyes, the nose ring, and the snarky quirk to his lips. It had all been too much up close, combined with the knowledge of what he looked like under his clothes. With the most random burst of *fuck this* confidence, I'd kissed him, for the first time in my entire life shutting off the voice that suspiciously sounds like my father's, talking about the queer perversions of the age. Talking about gay men ruining everything. Talking about sins against God.

For that whole thirty blissful seconds, I'd been free.

Then he'd touched my dick and brought me crashing back to the most painful reality I've ever experienced.

I didn't know kissing could be like that.

I didn't know I could want a person as much as I wanted him.

Even knowing he didn't hook up with that other man, I can't shake the sludgy, sickening jealousy that hit when I saw them walk off together. Because there will be other men. Plenty, apparently, and none of those men will be me.

Still, I wish I'd at least gotten his name.

You know. To make avoiding him easier.

I get home and strip out of my clothes as soon as I'm in my room, needing the cool air on my skin. A few of my brothers are hanging out in the house who didn't go to the party—mostly the ones who need to be serious about their studies. There aren't many of us who aren't already set up for life, and we try to be respectful of the others by not having all our parties here.

Given I need to take the bar, I still have to study my ass off and can't get everything through pure nepotism, but *if* that fell through, it wouldn't matter to me like it would to most. I'd still have my millions to fall back on.

At least, *straight* Archie would.

If Father found out I'd kissed another man tonight … the weight of his disappointment and disgust hits as heavily as if he was here. This is why, no matter how good it felt or how desperately I want to hunt that guy down again, I won't.

I'm smarter than that.

I flop back onto my bed and finally reach down to touch myself. I don't jerk off, just squeeze my length tighter and tighter, hoping to take the edge off.

That *damn* guy and the way he'd moaned. My lower lip still burns from where he bit it so hard, and it's like I can feel his hands sliding into my hair over and over again.

I bite my free fist, frustrated that I can't shake him. This isn't doing anything to help with my raging boner, and the last thing I'm going to do is jerk off to the memory and torture myself further.

I chose to be deep in the closet for a reason, and I've managed to keep the door locked my entire life. I've never even been tempted to peek outside at what I was missing because I already knew the answer: everything.

Part of my whole self stands outside the closet doors, and tonight, I think that part jumped right back in with me. It'd been way too much. Way too confronting.

There's a light knock on my door.

"Archie?"

I scramble for my sheet to throw over myself before I yell out to come in.

"Sup, brother," Steve says. "Thought I saw you come in, but then I was all, that can't be right, it's not even eleven."

"I wasn't feeling well."

"Damn. That's too bad because Lizzie wanted you to text her when you got in."

Without realizing it, Steve makes me feel even worse. Lizzie is a gorgeous girl. Exactly the type of girl Father wants me to walk away from college engaged to, and it's gotten to the point where he's been making regular visits to campus, trying to steal us both away for lunch in some weird attempt to get us together.

But it kills me every time we have sex. Not only because I put myself through it; I hate using her. Hate leading her on. Even though I know the likelihood of us being married in a few years is high. Once Father sets his mind to something, there's no saying no.

Even finding out his youngest son is gay wouldn't deter him.

"Thanks." I swallow and grab my phone. "I'll check in with her."

"Too easy, bro." Steve taps my doorframe twice before closing the door behind himself.

Needing to check in at all pisses me off. We're not dating. We're not anything other than resigned to a potential future together.

Instead of opening her number though, I roll over and pull a box out from under my bed that I've thrown the last few school newsletters into.

So much for forgetting tonight.

I flip through the pages, hating seeing my face over and over. I love the life I get to have here with my friends, but none of it feels … complete. Like no matter how much fun I'm having, I don't get to enjoy it. Don't get to let go and be free. It constantly feels like I'm having to remember to be careful, to play a part, to–

I freeze at the photo I've just come to.

Dash Lewis.

It's him. My mystery guy. Dash.

I kissed those lips barely an hour ago. Had his warm tongue in my mouth.

Imagining kissing a guy and actually doing it are two completely different things, and I don't know if all kisses with men are like that one was, but if they are, I've been missing out.

Big-time.

Which is why I'd been so determined to stay locked up and straight.

I'm not aware of when I start stroking myself, but it's no time before I'm hard and aching again. I stare at his photo, imagining being back in that hallway with him. Imagine him dropping to his knees. Licking his lips. Opening my fly and pulling me out.

My imagination gets as far as seeing Dash stick out his tongue and swipe it over my tip before it's too much. I come like a guy discovering his cock for the first time, and I want to scream, I'm so fucking mad at myself. Half for giving in to the urge and half for not making it last longer.

If I'm going to indulge, I should at least get the time to enjoy it.

My high drizzles away, and I sag back into the mattress, wiping my hand and cock off with my sheets before kicking them to the foot of the bed.

This whole situation blows.

And it's all because of Dash.

That asshole and his stupid drunken striptease.

I had a weak night.

Nothing more.

It's a big campus. There's no reason whatsoever for me to see him again.

Except to ask if he saw the crown I dropped.

Fuck.

Fine.

So, I ask him about that and that only, *and then* there's no reason to see him again.

I wonder if I can send one of the pledges to do it instead.

3

Dash

"WHERE'D YOU GO?" LARRY ASKS, LOCKING THE FRONT door of our apartment behind us. "Spoiler alert: I went swimming, and now this earache has only gotten worse."

"You make shitty decisions when you're drunk. Go figure." Like I'm one to talk.

He heaves his backpack further up his back and starts the walk toward campus. "Made out with a total ten though. Tits like this." He makes a hand motion in front of his chest.

"I'm so happy for you?" I try to imagine his reaction if I were all, "dude had balls like *this*," and mimed holding two bowling balls between my legs. Not gonna test that out though.

"What about you?"

"Eh, no luck." Not that I didn't have my chances. Instead, I chose to hang around that party like a bad smell, hoping Levine would hunt me down to get his crown back, but I didn't see him again. I wouldn't be surprised if he avoided me after his kiss since the guy is so deeply closeted.

It sucks knowing I have a chance but don't actually.

We reach campus, and Larry splits off for the science department while I head toward the math buildings. I fucking love studying economics, which is good because my whole being here is dependent on good grades. I'm smashing my classes, I'm smashing my social life, and once college is done with, I can get serious about life, but for right now, I've got a Kappa crown, and I'm going to be using it to pull at parties this weekend.

What better way to grab attention and start a conversation?

I ignore the fact that I'm after very specific attention and pretend to myself that anyone will do.

Like my thoughts have summoned him, I hear his rich-boy voice before I see him.

"You have my crown."

Well, look at that. I didn't even need to be wearing it to catch his attention. "Careful, someone might see you talking to me."

He glances around. "I don't care."

"Right. Sure you're not drunk again?"

He goes to bite back and shakes his head instead. "I need it back. Today, preferably."

"Might help if I knew what you were talking about."

"The one I was wearing and dropped when we … talked."

"Ah. *That* crown."

"Yes. And I need it back."

I shrug like there's nothing I can do, getting a sick satisfaction from taunting him into continuing this conversation. "I've invoked the age-old lore of finders keepers. There's nothing *I* can do."

"I'm not playing."

"Finders keepers isn't a game."

"Look, Dash—"

I gasp and hate that I do it. "You know my name."

His jaw tics. "Yes … well, you know, you did get naked. And people talk."

"That almost sounds like you were stalking me."

"I wasn't stalking anyone," he snaps. It's hot. Levine is so proper and put together it's fun to see little cracks in that facade.

"Yet you know my name without me telling you. Let's face it, you're basically obsessed at this point."

"Crown. I'm here for my crown."

"I think you mean *my* crown."

"No, I—" He cuts off and takes a long inhale. "Fine. What do you want?"

"Want?"

"Yes. Money? Name your price."

I turn to him so fast I get whiplash. "Wait, are you … You're serious."

"Obviously."

"Fine. One million dollars."

The choking sound he lets out is glorious. "Be serious."

"I am serious."

"It's a piece of plastic."

"Okay, so go and buy another piece of plastic. I'm sure you can find one with all the exact Kappa insignia on it that yours has."

His nostrils flare. "I'm going into law, and you've picked the worst person to mess with. What you're doing is illegal. Stealing."

"I told you—"

"There's no precedent for finders keepers. That's not actually something that will hold up in court."

"Oooh, so now you're taking me to court over the piece of plastic?"

He abruptly stops walking, fingers burying into his hair. "Why are you making this so difficult?"

"I like annoying people." It's true, especially when he scowls. "And let's face it, we both know you need an excuse to talk to me."

"Excuse me?"

I keep walking, and he scrambles to catch up. "You said it yourself. The crown is basically worthless, so the only *real* reason you're asking for it back is because you want to be able to approach me."

"Or maybe it's because my brothers will question me endlessly about it."

"Nah, I like my theory better."

"This conversation is anything but enjoyable, so I can promise you that's not it."

"Really? I'm having fun." I pause outside the math department and turn to look at him. Fuck me, he doesn't get any less hot. It should be a rule that as soon as a guy locks his cock in the closet, he immediately loses his appeal.

It would make things a lot easier on me.

His gorgeous eyes are wide. "I just need it back. Can you stop messing with me?"

"Why?"

"Because if they start asking questions about where I left it and how *you* ended up with it …"

"You really think they'll jump to the conclusion that you wanted me to suck your dick?"

"Shh." He glances around. "Keep your voice down."

"Literally nobody has ever given a shit about me before, so I don't know why you're freaking out."

"Because—"

"You're you? And people care about the great Archibald Levine."

His tongue swipes his lips. "Well. *You* certainly do. You think I'm great?" He cracks a smile. "Stop flirting with me."

Ooh, that's an opening. It's the universal way of telling someone that you do, in fact, want them flirting with you. I love that kind of opening, but with him … I hesitate. I've dreamed of having his attention for way too long, but this guy is going to fuck with my head. That isn't a guess; it's a guarantee. The real question is whether I'm going to let him.

And whether fucking with his head in return will be a worthy trade-off.

The thing is, if Levine is closeted, he has his reasons. I don't want to risk outing him, I don't want to push things, but a chance to hook up? To get to fulfill every fantasy I've ever had over the guy, no matter how slim the chance?

I'm a selfish, weak man and can't let the chance slip by.

"Maybe I like flirting with you."

Delicious red splotches rise over his cheeks, and when he talks again, it's softer. "I just need the damn crown."

"Don't sound very convincing."

"Please?"

I can't resist. "How did you know a cute guy begging is my weakness?"

"*Dash.*" He hangs his head back with a groan.

"Hey, you started it."

"I certainly did not."

"You're either lying or adorably oblivious. Either way, I can work with that."

"There is no working with anything. I'm not … not …"

I wait him out.

"It should never have happened."

"Liked it that much, huh?"

"Why are you so difficult?"

"Part of my charm."

Levine scruffs another hand through his glossy, copper curls. Fuck, his hair looks as soft as it felt the other night, and it's a crime if I never get to feel that again. "I have to get to class."

"Me too."

Neither of us makes a move.

"Can I come by and pick it up later?" he asks.

I'm tempted to play dumb, but even I know that's pushing things too far. "Put your number in here." I hand over my phone.

Levine hesitates a second before doing it. Then he calls himself. "Done."

"I guess I'll see you later, then."

"I guess you will." He hurries to clarify. "Just so I can pick up what belongs to me."

What would he say if he knew my fantasies belonged to him too?

"See you in a few hours."

"Okay." He turns to leave, and I can't stop myself.

"My roommate's working late."

Levine's long footsteps falter, but he pushes through and disappears around the corner before replying.

Then, because I want to make sure he knows where I stand, I pull out my phone and text: *U r so cute when u blush.*

I almost swallow my tongue when he replies.

Fuk u I'm cute always.

Jesus. Just when I thought I was the one in control of this thing, he's gotta go knocking my expectations out of the park. I want to text back. Desperately want to see if I can draw more flirting out of him, but that annoying niggle of self-preservation reminds me of what this is.

I'm not the type of guy people come out for.

It's cool with me; I've never wanted to be the take-home kind, especially when it comes to someone like Levine. His frat brothers make me uncomfortable enough, let alone older versions of them. Let alone *homophobic* older versions of them.

And if I'm not the kind of dude he'd be ready to get serious with, then I'm definitely not going to be tempting enough for him to risk being outed over. Still, a guy can dream, can't he?

Levine hasn't been able to stop me yet.

Almost as soon as I tuck my phone away, it goes off in my pocket. I walk into the lecture room and find a place off to the side where I can pull my phone out without drawing attention. Sure enough, it's him again.

No smartass comment 2 that. I'll take it as confirmation.

You know what? Fuck it. If Levine is going to get flirty with me, why should I be the one holding back?

I thought ur existence was ur confirmation of being king of the world?

Levine:

It's nice 2 be reminded I'm right.

Me:

Happy 2 be of service 2 ur ego.

Levine:

Thank u. My ego does love a good servicing.

I let my laugh sneak past my lips, glad he's not here to witness it. While normally flirting comes to me as easily as breathing, when I look at his messages, when I imagine those long fingers typing out his replies, the pressure piles on. I *want* him to like me. To be impressed by me. To maybe find me so damn irresistible that he can't hold back from fucking my lights out. I'm not his type, given the gorgeous, rich women he dates, but hey, maybe he wants to slum it for a night?

I'm down for that.

Me:

What about the rest of u?

I set my phone down and try to concentrate on the professor and not the lack of messages on my phone. Probably a good thing since I can't afford to text back and forth all day, but it doesn't stop me from worrying. Did I push too far? Is this past the limits of his comfort?

And mostly, more importantly, why do I care so much?

4

Archie

I clutch my pen tighter and tighter all through class and until we let out. I can't reply. I just can't do it. Because if I text one more word to Dash, it's going to be something I won't be able to laugh off as stupid banter.

I'm painfully attracted to him. It was hard being around him this morning, trying to focus on the fact that all I wanted was that stupid crown when I couldn't care less about that. All I care about is kissing him again.

My memory has to have amped up that moment to more than it was because there's no way a kiss could have moved my world as seismically as that one did. I don't care how good he is at it, the haze of wistfulness, of wanting, has created a memory that he could never live up to.

But fuck do I want to see him try.

All day, I type out a reply and chicken out again. It's easier to talk, to flirt, through text, and deep down, I want him to know I'm interested. Want him to know I'd do anything to kiss him again, but I can't get out of my head.

Without that freedom to know that I'd follow through on all my flirting, is there any point? This afternoon, I'll stop by and pick up the crown, then what? Then nothing.

He's right that I'll have no reason to talk to him again. It'd be safer that way.

My whole life, I've been safe. I've played by the rules and done as I was told and ticked all the metaphorical boxes needing to be ticked to get to a successful place in life. But now, this mystery box has been plunked in my path, and I don't think I'm strong enough to resist it.

Kissing him at a party was one thing. Trying it again, without the excuse of alcohol to fall back on?

Fuck, I don't even know this guy. There's no guarantee he won't spread my sexuality all over the campus, even if he hasn't already. I can't trust him. I can't be sure he's not showing my texts to people. It's that bitter reality that has me slipping my phone in my pocket and ignoring it for the rest of the day.

It's not until I wrap up my final class that I pull it out and text one question:

Where r u?

I'm a pressure valve of nerves while I wait for him to reply. What if he doesn't? What if he's already tired of my games and flat out refuses to give me my crown? I can't have that. Can't have him ghosting me.

I'm vibrating out of my skin as I pace, sure I look unhinged and not sure that I care all that much. I'm struggling to see the appeal though. Struggling to figure out what it is about the dark-haired, scruffy smart-ass that I can't get out of my head. He's not the most attractive man I've ever seen. He's definitely not the best dressed, and from the few conversations we've had, I can't imagine he's all that well-read or sophisticated either.

Being the first man I've seen completely naked who then hit on me is probably my reason for all this obsessing. It's definitely not his rough hands or his deep eyes or the way his top lip forms a perfect bow shape.

It's easy enough to resist those things, even if I don't particularly want to.

His reply makes my gut trip over itself.

Bean and Gone. South side of campus.

Well, there goes this morning's flirting. Thankfully.

I head for the coffee shop, building my confidence for when I see him again. There's no way I'm letting some guy intimidate me. At least that's what I tell myself until I actually lay eyes on him again.

Oh, holy fuck. Why am I so goddamn attracted to all that?

His backpack is hanging off one shoulder, headphones

slung around his neck, and the logo stretched across his chest looks like it's from some band or another. His sneakers are scuffed up, and his nose ring is prominent, but the second he spots me, those lips curl into a sinful smile that I feel right to my knees.

Goddamn, Levine, you're better than this.

I straighten out my shoulders and approach, stealing the coffee from his grip before he can stop me. "Thanks." Whatever he's drinking is bitter, but I choke it down anyway.

"Sure. Help yourself."

"You stole from me. I thought it was a thing we did."

"Well, you sure taught me a lesson." Dash rolls his eyes and starts walking across campus. I have to force myself not to hurry after him like a lost puppy. That's not me. That's not who I want to be. I keep my strides measured and confident, and eventually, Dash slows slightly. It might be a small win, but I'll take it.

"So," he gets out between his teeth. "Good classes?"

"Eh, they were fine." I glance over at his scruffy hair, hating how much that look is doing it for me. "What about you?"

"Would have been easier to concentrate if I'd gotten a reply from the guy I've been hitting on." He throws me a grin, and I can't help my laugh.

"Fucking hell."

"That's been my same thought all day."

"Are you trying to give me an aneurysm?"

"Actually, I'd rather give you an orgasm, but I can try to give you one of those too."

My cheeks are getting hot, which means I'm blushing. I got a lot of good things from the Levine gene pool, but easy blushing I could have done without. It sucks being powerful, wealthy, headed into criminal law, and not being taken seriously because I blush like a five-year-old over a Disney prince.

And damn does Dash have a hobo *Eric* look going on.

"Still on about that, are you?" I ask, my voice a notch deeper than before.

"Sex is never far from my mind."

"Well, you should probably at least stop hitting on straight men."

When he smiles, his whole face lights up. "Ah, yes. The straight man who chased off my hookup and kissed me. All totally unplanned, obviously, which is why he was carrying my T-shirt around with him."

"I'm starting to think that crown isn't worth it."

"Of course it isn't." He sinks his teeth deep into his bottom lip as he runs his eyes from my face to my feet. "Why are you closeted?"

"I'm not—"

"Cut the shit, Levine. I've seen the way you look at me. I've read your texts. You have no reason to believe I'm not going to spread that around, but I have no interest in outing you. The world is fucked, and honestly, the less guys who know you're on the table, the better." He pumps his dark eyebrows my way. "The way I see it, you can answer my question and talk about it with someone who knows, or you can keep pretending, and I'll pretend to keep pretending like I believe you."

I snort. "When have you once pretended to pretend you believe me?"

"In my defense, it's a difficult one to fake convincingly."

I hate that he doesn't let things go like a normal person would. Doesn't he understand that there are some things you can talk about and some things you can't? If someone is clearly closeted, you're supposed to sweep that conversation under the rug, not drag it kicking and screaming into a topic of conversation.

"I was closeted in high school," he says. "I get it. There are reasons. I'm going to go out on a limb here and guess your family."

It takes me a moment to make up my mind. "My dad."

Dash's face loses some of that superiority, and real emotion shines through for the first time. That real emotion might be goddamn pity, but beggars can't be choosers. "He a homophobic dickweed?"

"Basically. He doesn't say too much publicly, but behind closed doors …" I shudder at some of the things that have come from that man's mouth. "Let's just say that being me was never an option."

"Damn."

"It is what it is. I have basically everything else in life; it seems selfish to want that too."

"It's not a want though, is it? Are you gay? Bi?"

I'm hesitant to say too much out loud.

He nods. "Gay, then."

My breath comes out in a rush. "Can we move to a new conversation?"

"Sure. If you hang around for dinner?"

"What?" That's the last thing I expected him to say.

"I told you my roommate works late, and who else do you have to talk to about this? Any of your fratty bros?"

"Ah, no. There's …" I hate admitting this. "You're the only one who knows."

He fist pumps. "Sucks for you, but the way I see it; you've gotta stay for dinner now. It's like the lore of the finders keepers. I'm your gay Obi-Wan, and you're my grasshopper."

"Padawan. Not grasshopper. That analogy was painful to listen to."

"Your whole life is painful to witness, but you don't hear me whining about it. Dinner? Yes? Good."

I know what I want to do, and I know what I should do. *Should* would be grabbing my crown and running. *Want* is take his offer and see where it leads. The thing is, he's not really offering is he? It's more of a demand. And who am I to say no to the man?

My gut is in knots when I ask, "What are you cooking me?"

"Cooking? Calm down, fancy pants. I'm talking about ordering pizza."

"Pizza?"

"Tell me you know what that is."

"Of course I know what it is, but can't we go with Thai or something?"

"I'm paying and have about twenty bucks to my name. You're going to have to get used to slumming it, big guy."

I could argue about the paying thing because I have a lot more than twenty dollars, but something else he's said catches my attention. "Ah, 'used to'?"

"After one night, you're going to be hooked on me. I don't make the rules."

"Well, why don't we see if we can make it through the one night first? I'm about ninety percent sure I'll have the urge to strangle you instead."

"It's a fine line, Levine," he says. "But I can guarantee by the end of the night, you'll want your hands on me. One way or another."

5

Dash

I REFUSE TO ACT NERVOUS AS I LEAD ARCHIBALD LEVINE the Third into my apartment, which hardly has enough room to swing a cat. I'm not usually a guy with a lot of pride, but I can't stop the way I straighten, braced to defend my living arrangements.

Levine passes me and drops onto the couch that we picked up for fifteen bucks at a flea market. The afternoon sun is struggling to make it through the yellowed windows, and okay, if he had something to say, I'd get it, but thankfully, he's keeping his trap shut. I hover for a second, wondering if I should offer him a drink, or … how the hell do people do this? I'm so glad I don't date.

Levine lifts his eyebrows, looking as comfortable here as he does at one of his frat parties. "My crown?"

"Answer me this first: are you going to ditch as soon as you get it?"

"How can I? You offered me pizza."

"I knew it was the right choice."

I duck into my room off the kitchen, trying to make myself breathe properly, and grab the plastic crown that feels like so much more than a stupid memento. Fuck, am I glad I picked it up that night. Before I leave my room, I check my hair, cringe as I realize it's way past needing a cut and I can't do anything with it, then give my shirt a quick sniff.

Mmm, stale sweat.

Shit.

I strip off my shirt and toss it into the corner, then hunt around for something clean. This could be it. My one shot. I'm going to flirt, but it'll be up to him to make the first move since he's here but hesitant. Wanting but too afraid to take.

There's no risk for me except letting the guy I can't get out of my fantasies slip through my fingers. On my way back out, I hesitate in the kitchen, then grab two beers before I can overthink it. It's what I'd do for any friend who visited, and at this point, I could really use having something else to concentrate on than Levine's mouth. His curls. Those broad shoulders.

I grunt and try to rid all that from my mind.

"Here." I hold out the bottle, and he takes it gratefully. Hopefully, it's because he needs as much liquid courage as me and not that he's, like, an alcoholic. Neither of us is stupid. We both know there's an attraction; we both know the other wants sex. But neither of us knows how to get to that point.

"Ever kissed a guy before me?" I ask, taking the seat next to him. I've never been happier about our cramped little apartment in my life.

Levine chokes on the sip of beer. "I thought we were starting a new conversation."

"This is," I protest. "We've moved on from homophobic families to past experiences."

"That's not what I meant when I said new topic." His embarrassed smile is adorable. "I thought we'd talk football, or politics, or—"

I groan. "You really want to talk about any of those things?"

His gorgeous eyes meet mine again, and he's not doing anything to hold back the want there. "Y-yes?"

"Fine." I smirk when he doesn't hold back his disappointment either. "Which football players do you want to bang?"

The laugh he lets out is clearly unexpected. "Jesus, Dash."

I set his crown between us, and the amusement slowly dies on his face. He's got it now. There's absolutely no reason why he can't make up an excuse to leave. He stares at it for so long I'm worried he's stroked out, but then he picks it up and leans forward to set it on the coffee table.

Levine turns his whole body toward me, elbow rested on the back of the couch. "Do you think it's odd that all those players wear such tight tights? Then there's that one guy with his face in his teammate's ass and hand right up in his business, but all the dude bros think it's the greatest thing they've ever seen in their lives?"

"Pretty sure that player is the QB and everyone's favorite."

Levine's lips twitch. "An actual gay icon."

"Jerk off about him a lot, do you?"

He shakes his head, but the blush is a dead giveaway.

"You filthy boy. You totally get off on the hot football players—look at how red you are."

"You're making me want to get up and leave."

I light up at the way his eyes dip to my lips. "No one's stopping you."

"You're so fucking irritating."

"It's what gets all the boys hot."

Levine huffs and turns back to his beer bottle, wrapping his lips around it and drinking deeply. I don't like how quickly it's going down.

"You getting drunk again, huh?"

"No."

"You sure? Because your version of drunk and my version of drunk are two very different things."

I swear steam bursts from his nose. "This is a big thing for me."

"What is?" I taunt.

He drinks more, then sets the glass bottle down heavily. "This."

Levine doesn't give me a chance to react when he grabs my shirt and hauls me his way. Our mouths crash together, and pure lust threatens to short-circuit my brain. He's as confident and commanding as last time, confirming my suspicions that Levine might be nervous and unsure, but he's been raised to be comfortable in any situation he finds himself in.

And right now, he's finding himself under me.

I get my head straight and throw one leg over his thighs, fingers delving into the curls I can't get enough of. They're as silky as last time, twisting around my fingers and making my cock ache. I don't dare touch it though. Don't dare bring us any closer than we are. Touching him was the thing that brought him back to reality last time, and this time, I'm not making that mistake again. His dick is off-limits until he says it isn't.

All I want is to focus on his mouth anyway.

Whether he's kissed a guy before or not, he knows what he's doing. His tongue licks into my mouth, jaw stretched like he's melding us together, and the pure want is getting me so riled up I can barely stand it. Each kiss, each moan, each time he licks my lip and then sucks it into his mouth ... I'm trying to work out if this feels like pure fire because I've been picturing it for so long or because my body knew our chemistry would be off the charts, but I don't think I'll get over this kiss for as long as I live.

A hand settles on my waist. The warmth from his palm thrills me, and even through his hesitance, he squeezes, grips tighter, finally letting his fingers dip under the hem and meet skin. It's like I can feel him pushing for more, read the way he's forcing himself to cross those lines, and it's only when he does that, he realizes how fucking amazing it feels.

His other hand isn't as hesitant. It dives under the front of my shirt, splaying over my abs, fingertips dancing over the impressions. His wrist is hovering right over my cock, and all I'd need to do to make contact is tilt my hips forward.

It's painful to hold back, but if I'm reading him right, and I'm sure I am, he needs this. Needs me to let him explore and feel out his boundaries, and if those boundaries lead to more touching, I'm not going to complain.

My mind is mushy from the kiss when he suddenly jerks back.

His hands don't move, but when my eyes flick open, I find him looking up at me. Rapid breaths pass between his kiss-swollen lips, his eyes that clear bluey-green that the ocean goes on a perfect day.

"I've never kissed a man before."

My lips kick up on one side. "I figured."

"I know you did. I know you've also probably guessed, uh …"

"That you're a virgin?"

He frowns. "No. I've had sex plenty of times before, but …"

"Wait. So, you're not gay?"

"I am." He shakes his head, and I know where he's going with this. Also know I don't want to hear it.

"It was just with—" Before he can say more, I take over.

"You've never had real sex before," I say, hand slipping from his hair down his neck. "Never felt this rush of want." I play with the top of his shirt before resting my hand over his chest. "Never felt the way your heart might beat out of your chest because you're so excited. The way your blood burns for that little bit more." I lean in closer, and his mouth immediately tilts up for me, but I don't kiss him. My knuckles run between his pecs and down his abs. "You feel me in here, don't you? Deep, deep down, there's that ball of need. That topsy-turvy feeling telling you that if you don't touch me, you'll die."

He hisses as I drop my hand lower. Fingers trailing across the top of his Calvin Kleins.

"But most of all, you've never felt the ache in your cock that you do right now. Never felt the way it wants to explode. Wants to be touched. Wants my wet mouth wrapped around it."

"Fuck, Dash."

My stubble scrapes his as I dip my mouth to his ear. "Take off your shirt."

He does it automatically, like he's on strings. As soon as it's gone, he goes to close the distance between us again, but I hold back.

"Now take off mine."

Levine's pupils expand, gaze dropping from my face to my chest. This time, he's slower, throat bobbing as he swallows and reaches for the bottom. "This is so weird," he mutters.

"Why? I might be a guy, but you've undressed people before, I'm assuming."

This time when he meets my stare, his eyes hold a vulnerability I never thought I'd see in him. "Nothing like this …" He doesn't look away as he pushes my shirt up and over my head. The exhale he lets out as he takes me in is strained and pinches something in my chest.

I'm so tempted to snark that no one is like me, so that checks out, but I bite my tongue. I've never been uncomfortable during sex before, so this might be a first, but it has nothing to do with the sex itself and everything to do with how he's looking at me.

"So much hotter up close," he rasps.

"You should see me naked up close." The words slip out before I catch them, and I internally cringe at the thought I've fucked this all up. So much for taking it slow and letting him lead. No, my stupid brain wants my stupid cock out as fast as stupidly possible.

"Can I?"

The question catches me totally off guard, especially with the tone it's asked in. This time, I'm the one not sure how the hell to move forward here because I'd strip us both off in a second, no worries; I'm just not so sure he's ready for that. "How many dicks have you seen?"

"Outside of porn?" A flash of teeth with his quick smile. "Just yours. And you were whipping that thing around way too fast for me to get a good look."

"And you want a good look now?"

His nod is slow but determined.

I climb off Levine's lap. "Well, come on, then. Let's go and get naked."

6

Archie

MY EYES ARE GLUED TO DASH'S ASS AS HE LEADS THE way to his bedroom. He said his roommate isn't back until later, but having this extra layer of privacy does a lot to settle my nerves. He's too far away as he crosses the kitchen and reaches his bedroom, but even if he wasn't, would it matter? The thought of touching him is an impossible one. I'm so tempted though.

Dash watches me, one hand on his door and the other hanging relaxed by his side as I approach. He's so smugly confident, knows I'm way out of my depth here, but all that does is turn me on more. I'd been ready to rut against

him until I came in my pants on the couch, but I'm so glad
I got up the courage to ask for more.

I want him naked.

Need it.

More than I've ever needed anything in my life.

I step through into his room, and Dash closes the door
behind me.

"What now?" I ask.

"You wanted me naked, right?"

I don't trust myself to speak.

Dash moves next to his bed, then stands there, staring
at me. "Get me naked, then."

"You want me to undress you?"

"Sure do."

God fucking dammit, Archie, you can do it. If I can
strip off a woman I have no interest in, I can sure as hell
unwrap the package making my mouth water. All it will
take is a tiny bit of courage for me to get to have a
moment I've only ever dreamed about.

My feet are heavy, but I force them toward him. "You
sure you won't tell anyone about this?"

"Promise."

There's no reason for me to believe him, but I do. "I'll
probably never get to do this again," I whisper.

"Way to put pressure on a guy."

"Sorry, but … I shouldn't even be doing this now. A
second time …" I shake my head, not able to picture it.
So, if I'm doing this and it won't happen again, I need to

kick my nerves to the curb and let myself enjoy the moment.

"No repeats. It's fine. It's not something I do a lot of anyway," he says. "You don't need excuses to blow me off. This is just sex, Levine."

"Archie."

"What?"

"If we're going to have sex, you can at least get my name right."

He looks like he's trying not to laugh at me. "Get your ass over here, Archie."

I don't stop until our toes are almost touching, and then I glance down to where the front of his pants is stretched tight over him. My cheeks are hot as I reach out and undo his button. Slide down the zipper.

My mouth dries with how fast I'm breathing.

"It's not going to bite you."

"Keep making fun of me and I'll bite you."

"I know you're new to this, but that isn't much of a threat."

"This is a lot for me."

"I know. It's adorable."

"Fuck you."

Dash snickers. "Wish you would, but you're taking forever."

It's pure irritation alone that makes me plunge my hand into the front of his pants and wrap my hand around his cock. It feels nothing like mine. Still smooth skin and straining hardness, but he's thicker, curves more, and, well, it's not my cock. Knowing that is the biggest difference, and the surge of lust it floods me with is helping take my nervousness away.

I push down his pants, briefs and all, and then I get to work on stripping off too.

I don't dare to look at him until I'm completely naked, and then I shove him backward onto the bed.

His pale skin stands out against the navy bedspread, dark hair a wild mess, as he watches me with a wide grin, legs splayed to the side, and all of that gorgeous body in view for me.

Everything about him is hard angles. His pecs, his sharp collarbones, the muscles in his shoulders and thighs, and then his steely hard cock, curving up toward his belly button.

I get a rush of something so powerful I almost pass out.

"Fuck," I breathe.

"You haven't even seen my ass yet."

"Not sure I'd survive it, honestly."

Dash gives himself a stroke, and the noise that leaves me barely sounds human.

"Let me make this easy for you," he says. "I'm going to count to three, and by the time I get there, I want you on top of me. One, two—"

Before he can hit three, I climb onto the bed and cover

him in one smooth motion. Our mouths meet as he chuckles, and then I lower my weight onto him.

All our hot, bare skin presses together. Cocks lined up. Legs tangled.

"Nmfuck," he moans into my mouth, and knowing that Dash feels as good as I do spurs me on. I roll my hips against his and want to sob at how amazing it feels. That I've waited so long for this and will probably never get the courage to do it again in my life.

Dash feels incredible beneath me. Everything about him turns me on, from his leg hair to his pubes to his muscle and the light hair on his chest. He's got an aggressiveness about the way he kisses and twists his hands in my hair, and I try to match him on that level. I'm holding up my weight on one side, so I only have one hand to work with, but with a bravery I didn't know I have, it settles on his bare side, then slowly trails down and around to his ass.

He didn't lie about having a great ass.

I break from the kiss, dropping my head to taste his neck instead. He's fucking delicious. Addictive. I breathe deeply, drinking in his scent and the subtle fragrance of his shampoo. Something nutty.

My mouth closes over the soft skin where his neck meets his shoulder, and Dash lets out a gasp.

"More of that."

"You like?"

"Duh. I'm not dead. Suck harder."

"What if I give you a hickey?"

His laugh is low and husky. "Then you give me a hickey. I'm not the one who's closeted, remember?"

What that must be like, to be able to hook up with all the men I wanted and having none of the regret. Because I can guarantee when I leave here that I'm going to regret it. A lot.

My grip on his ass tightens, and I move faster on top of him. Another dick against mine is the single hottest thing I've ever experienced, and I don't know how I can go back after knowing—as Dash put it—what real sex is.

It's not the act. It's not about parts. It's about this feeling, this need, that's completely overtaken me as I share my body with him.

We're both leaking precum, making the movement between us easier. My balls have tightened, and each thrust is getting rougher, more erratic, bringing our cocks together with force.

Dash's hands drop to grip my ass cheeks, steadying himself as he meets my rhythm. Our bodies work together, no space between us, both of us panting, even as I shiver at how tight my skin prickles around me.

I release his ass and grip his throat instead, bringing our foreheads together. I'm too out of breath to kiss him, too close to the edge to stop, but looking down into his face helps me remember this is happening, and it's a moment I never want to forget.

"Are you close?" I rasp, wanting to make sure this isn't all in my head.

He nods in my hold. "Just about there. Keep going."

I double up my efforts, not ready to end this but needing to. I'm so blindingly horny I forget to be worried or nervous or hold back. All I can think of is how I'd give anything to be able to experience this again.

"Don't look away," I tell him. "Say my name when you come."

"What?"

"*Say it.*"

His hips rock frantically against mine, knees bracketing my hips, sweat building between our flushed torsos. "So, so close," he chants. "So close. Just need … just a bit …"

His eyes roll back as sticky cum releases between us, and when he opens his mouth, "*Archie …*" falls out on a groan.

The flicker of possessiveness lights up my gut, and my hold on his throat tightens. I'm working my way closer, toeing the edge, ready to fall, when Dash flips us so suddenly, I'm not ready for it.

My back hits the mattress, and my cock cries out at the lack of friction, but before I can complain, Dash leans forward and swallows my cock to the back of his throat.

"Fuck!" My head arches back at the pleasure as I grip his sheets for dear life. Dash doesn't take it easy on me. He gives me the fastest, sloppiest, hottest blow job I've ever had, and the heat and suction of his mouth is heaven. I thrust up into it, sinking in the bliss filling my limbs, chasing a high that's already beyond anything I've ever experienced.

I linger on the edge, fighting my orgasm and knowing it's a losing battle. Dash makes me feel way too good.

"Now," I warn him. "I'm gonna—"

He swallows around me, and I let go. My cock thickens before throbbing my release out into his throat, and Dash takes it all. Like he's greedy for it. Hungry. And when I glance down and our eyes clash, he doesn't look away.

When I'm done, he slowly releases me, tongue dragging along my length until I slip from his mouth.

"Well." I'm at a loss for words. "Wow."

"I'll say." He flops down beside me, head propped up on his hand. "Do you know I could taste my cum on your dick? Talk about hot."

Even after what we just did, I somehow manage to blush. "That was … okay?"

"I didn't tell you this before, but I've been wanting to bed you for a while now. You're a hard guy not to notice, and I can guarantee that it didn't matter what we did, I was always going to enjoy it."

"You knew I was gay?"

"No clue. Figured it was hopeless. Didn't make me any less attracted to you though."

I roll onto my side and mirror how he's lying. "How long is a while?"

"I dunno. Last year sometime?"

"Interesting …"

"What is?"

I flick his nipple, just wanting to touch it. "How hot you are for me."

"No shame from me." He punches the air. "Thank fuck for that strip show."

"I could say the same." There's a silence where I'm not sure if I'm supposed to get up and leave or not.

"Come on," Dash says, throwing his legs off the side of the bed. "Get dressed, and we'll order. Pizza, beer, and checking out football players in their tights sounds like the perfect way to end our night."

I hate to admit he might be onto something there.

7

Dash

Weekends come and go, I head to parties, and I head home solo. The only changes to my schedule are that first, I make sure Levine won't be at any of them, and second, I haven't hooked up with anyone since him.

It's a fucking issue. The sex was supposed to tick that little conquest box so I could move on to others.

It hasn't.

It's only made everything worse.

If I'd known Archie Levine was going to be *this* much of a pain in the ass, I would have avoided those frat parties at all costs. Sometimes a pretty face isn't worth it. I wasn't even this cockblocked when I was closeted.

"Holy shit, look at this," Larry says, tearing a flyer off a pole as we walk past. "Sounds like it'll be a good laugh."

"What is it?"

"Jousting night at Kappa."

"What the hell is that?"

"Just says the theme is medieval and the fraternities are going to have some kind of joust battle." He chuckles. "I'm down to see a bunch of drunken fraternity brothers injure each other."

Yeah, but one of those brothers is bound to be Archie, and I'm not ready to face him again.

"You have fun."

His eyes almost fall out. "There's no way you're leaving me to go to this thing by myself."

"Sure am. We don't hang out at parties together anyway."

"Yeah, but we show up together! Getting there alone is sad." His voice breaks it goes so high-pitched. "You love a good Kappa party."

"Yeah, a good one. That one looks terrible."

"You're lying through your ass. What's going on?"

I shrug, trying to play it off and definitely not skimming campus ahead of us for any familiar faces. "Just cooling off on the party scene."

"Another lie." Larry steps in front of me, trying to make his lanky, gawky form intimidating. "Did something happen?"

"Like what?"

"I don't know, that's why I'm asking."

Larry is a laid-back guy, so seeing him get protective like this is cute. It also makes me feel like shit for not being able to tell him anything. I meant my promise to Levine–I won't out him–which means my choices are to let my best friend worry or suck it up and go to a stupid party. Considering Larry won't notice if I duck out immediately, I probably won't have to face Archie at all. Simple.

"If it means that much to you, I'll go," I say, throwing my arm around his shoulders. "Wouldn't want my boy missing out on a chance to get drunk! What would all those college chicks do without you there to hit on?"

He shoves me off. "You're such a dick."

"Anything for my little buddy."

"I'm like half a foot taller than you."

"Still maintain you wear lifts."

"Whatever. See you for dinner." He forces the flyer into my hand and leaves.

I head toward the social sciences wing and glance down at the poster made of clip art and crazy letters.

The Princes of Kappa House Challenge Ye.

Fuck my life.

WHEN I AGREED TO COME TO THIS STUPID PARTY, I DIDN'T realize I'd be agreeing to getting dressed up as well. The worst part is that all the hot costumes were gone, so Larry and I had to rock, paper, scissors for the soldier costume, and I'd lost. Now, I'm in boots, tights, and a fucking tunic. The belt around my waist has a sword strapped to it, so if Levine *does* see me, at least I'll look a little bit tough.

The line to get into Kappa house is long, so Larry and I skip it and swing around to the back of the property. Between the high brick fence and some hedges, there's just enough room to shuffle through. Fuck paying ten a head to grace their party. Those assholes can afford what I drink in cheap booze, especially considering tonight, I'm not planning on drinking anything.

We sneak through the hedges—and I'm glad I didn't bother fixing my hair with how the bushes tug at it—and then skirt around the trees on the property border.

Only, instead of stepping into a backyard full of people drunkenly stumbling around, we step right into— the jousting path.

"Fuck!" I narrowly avoid being hit by a frat brother madly pedaling on a toddler's tricycle. He's holding a mop handle, while on the other side, another brother is stuffed into a kid's toy car, scooting at a speed that I wouldn't have guessed possible, with a feather duster out and ready.

Larry steps out of the tree line behind me, and I haul him against me and out of the way.

His cackle hits my ear. "I already love this party! Come on."

All I know is the two competitors aren't Levine, but he's likely around here somewhere. My eyes stay glued to the ground as I follow Larry up to the back of the main house. We grab drinks, and I expect him to split off from me, when he grabs my forearm and tugs me back toward the jousting. "Let's go watch."

"You go. I wanna dance."

He hurries to shake his head. "I can dance."

"You?"

"Sure? It's, uh, so fun."

For someone as wildly uncoordinated as him, I highly doubt he's suddenly gained a love of dancing. "What are you doing?"

"Enjoying the party."

"Larry …"

"Fine." He slumps. "You seemed worried about coming, so I didn't want to leave you alone."

I grin so hard I scare him. "That's a bit cute."

"Fuck off."

"You got my back, man. I appreciate it."

He scowls even as his neck goes red. "You don't have to be an asshole about it."

I laugh. "No, I'm actually serious."

"Whatever, Dash." He flips me off and leaves.

Reminding me that being nice to people gets you nowhere. I'm still laughing about it when someone presses flush to my back, and before I can shake them off, he speaks directly into my ear. "Who the fuck was that?"

Levine.

A shiver ripples down my spine, and flashes of the night we spent together immediately hit my memories.

Telling him Larry's my friend and roommate would be easy, but the growl in his tone has me feeling reckless. It's been too long since I've seen him, and apparently, the distance knocked out a few brain cells.

"My date."

His huff is so heavy it skirts down my neck. "Bullshit."

"Oh yeah?" I step aside so I can turn and see him, which isn't a smart move. He's wearing the crown again and is dressed as an actual prince this time. He goddamn suits it. Pure royalty. Even the eyeliner is getting me hard. I remember how easily he took over when we were together, and there's no denying why I've hit a dry spell.

Unfortunately for me, no guy on campus can match Archie Levine.

I steady my breathing, not wanting him to know how much he affects me. "You think I can't pull a guy like him?" I ask.

Levine's teeth clench as he reaches up and plucks a leaf out of my hair. "I saw you leave the bushes with him." He closes most of the distance between us, and I have the strangest urge to remind him that he's supposed to be closeted. "Did he suck your cock?"

"Why? Jealous you never did?"

Guilty pleasure comes in the form of his nostrils flaring. "You're really going to come to my house, my party, and hook up with men under my nose?" He shakes his head. "What the fuck, Dash?"

I'm feeling way too good about this. "Wow. It almost sounds like you're jealous, but that can't be right."

"I'm not jealous. It's called respect."

"Uh-huh. I love the way you *respectfully* came all over me."

Levine quickly glances around, but the music is too loud, and there are way too many people in here for anyone to pay us a second of attention. "You said you'd keep it secret, that you wouldn't—"

I pat his chest. "Big guy, if anyone is going to out you, it's *you.* You've got me all but pressed to the wall. We might as well be making out."

Surprisingly, he doesn't back up, just drops his gaze to the foot of distance between us before returning his glare to me. "I forbid you from hooking up with anyone else at my parties."

"*Forbid* me? What in the toxic fuck are you talking about?"

His hand *thumps* against the wall beside me. "If I can't hook up with anyone else, it isn't fair that you get to."

"Dude, you can hook up with whoever you want. I'm

not stopping you. And you're *not* stopping me. We agreed to one and done, you're off the table, so unless you're going to give it up again, you don't get to dictate who I can and can't sleep with."

"No, but I can have you thrown out."

My laugh is hollow. "I didn't even want to come to this stupid party."

"You didn't?"

"Of course not. I've been avoiding you."

"You have?" His face falls. "Guess that explains why I haven't seen you around."

I don't know why I keep giving him the time of day, but I don't walk away like I should. "Have you been looking?"

He doesn't answer.

"Hoping to bump into me on campus?"

His glare deepens.

"Thought you might trip out of your clothes and land on me again?"

I know I'm on the right track based on how he's looking at me. A mixture of want and regret.

"Dash …"

"All I'm saying is that I'm safe. A locked box. Really, really good at keeping secrets."

"You said repeats aren't something you do."

"Well—" My gaze flicks up to his crown. "—I can always make an exception for royalty."

Levine's eyes flare with heat, tongue flicking out to

wet his lips as he stares at me. It's like I can read his mind, and knowing he's tempted to sleep with me again is boosting my ego in a big way. Sure, this is sort of a "last man on earth" situation, but if that's what it takes for me to end up naked with him again, I'll take it.

"There you are!" Levine is yanked away from me as a pretty blond girl grabs his arm. Based on the way she giggles and falls against him, I get the feeling she's already had a few. "I've been looking for you."

I hate her instantly.

Mostly because I know I've seen her hanging off him at other parties and also because of the way he immediately smiles fondly right back.

My good mood immediately sours, and before he can forget my existence, I slip out from behind them and disappear into the party.

I know I should go home. I know there's nothing left at this party for me.

But goddamn, my ego can't take her winning.

Instead of heading for the front door like I'd planned, I hook a left down a hall lined with bedrooms and pull out my phone.

Me:

If you want me, come and find me.

8

Archie

"WHAT'S GOING ON, ARCHIE?" LIZZIE ASKS, RUNNING her hands over my chest. "You haven't texted me back all week."

There's no way for me to answer that without making us both feel like shit. Seeing Lizzie reminds me of how off the tracks my life has gotten and that I have no idea how to fix everything.

Starting at college, rushing Kappa house as a legacy, finding the perfect pseudo girlfriend, it was all part of a step-by-step guide on how to be the perfect Levine.

But now ... well, maybe perfect is overrated.

I glance back toward Dash, hoping he'll help me get

out of this situation, and my gut falls to find a blank stretch of wall where he was standing a minute ago.

Did he run off to find his date? Is he on the search for another guy to spend the night with?

I was clear that there wouldn't be a round two for us, but I'd … well, fuck. I'd sort of hoped he'd come begging. If he's there and he's desperate, I'd have to help him out with it. I wouldn't have a choice, really, and because I'm such a considerate person, we would have ended up sleeping together again.

Him actively *avoiding* me? Talk about a kick to the system.

The thing is, why shouldn't he? Dash is beautiful, and he doesn't have to worry about sneaking around. Why the hell would he waste time with me when he could probably have any guy on campus that he wanted?

Just that thought alone makes me see red.

Maybe it has something to do with him being the first man I've ever been with, but I can't shake him. He feels like mine, and the thought of another guy getting to enjoy him makes a dark possession churn in my gut. I've never had that with Lizzie; I've never had that with any woman. I don't think I've ever had that with any guy either.

I just know that I have to find him. Now.

"I have to go," I tell Lizzie.

She immediately frowns. "What the hell, Arch? What's going on?"

"I'm …" She's close with Dad, so I can't even tell her

the whole story. "I'm having second thoughts. I'm sorry, but this … it's not working out."

"*Excuse* me?"

I leave before she can say any more. The feelings were low on both sides, hence why she hasn't cared too much about my lack of contact, but the mutual knowledge of us getting engaged one day was always there.

Not anymore.

I might have to play straight, but I'm done with dragging her into it. I'm done with having to uncomfortably fulfill the lie. I'll die alone for all I care; for tonight, this moment, I want Dash. I want him so much it hurts.

My blood is pumping, my nerves are high, and my face is so goddamn hot from the rush of excitement at letting myself go for this. He'd made it clear he was interested; does that still hold true after seeing Lizzie?

My phone goes off, and when I pull it out and see his name on my screen, my pulse ramps up a notch.

Come find me.

I don't stop to think about it. I fly through the party, searching every fucking inch of the grounds and the house, sure he must be on the move too. As every minute ticks by, I get more and more frustrated, wanting to catch a glimpse of that messy hair or his twisted grin. My hands itch to hold his face, and I won't be satisfied tonight until my mouth is on his. I've tried to be good for weeks.

I failed.

Might as well jump in with both feet while I can.

Half an hour passes, and my frustration ramps up. Is he even here anymore? Is this all some sick joke?

If I find out he's left this party after texting me, I'm going to explode.

I shoulder my way past people as I take the hall to my bedroom, planning to lock myself in and call him. Only when I get the door open and step inside—

"Dash."

"About time you—"

I slam the door behind me and grab him in one movement.

He chuckles deeply. "Shouldn't we lock the door?"

"Fuck."

Dash steps around me, locks it, then instead of coming closer again, he leans back against the wood. He looks up at me from under messy black hair, held back by the bandana he has sitting across his forehead.

"You found me," he says.

"You told me to."

The smile that hitches one side of his lips makes my knees weak. "You always do what you're told?"

"Actually, I prefer to be the one making demands."

"Shocking news." Dash's dark eyes run over me. "What would you have me do, Your Majesty?"

Why does that go straight to my cock? And why, even when he's asking me to call the shots, does it feel like Dash is in control anyway?

The loose shirt he's wearing is open at the chest and

pulled in at the waist. His pants are tight, boots meeting his knees, and the casual way his hand is resting on that fake sword is doing it for me. For all of me.

I sink my teeth into my knuckles as I take him in. "You have no right to look that sexy."

He shifts the sword and holds his other hand out to the side. "This costume was literally my only option. Tell the truth—you only set the theme because you wanted to look all powerful and royal, didn't you?"

"I actually had nothing to do with this party, fuck you very much."

"You mean you didn't want to knock some of your brothers off their high horse?"

"No. I actually like the guys I live with."

"Like? Or *like* like? Which ones do you think are hot?"

"None." I'm serious about that. I've always been careful to keep my distance from other men and make sure not to tempt myself. I just didn't see Dash coming.

"You sure? The dude riding the tricycle when I showed up was hot."

My teeth clash together. "Straight."

"Yeah, but so were you. Maybe I like my chances."

I close the distance between us. "Stop trying to make me jealous."

"Why would I do that when it makes you look so hot?"

"Believe it or not, I don't find it all that enjoyable."

"Yeah, but I do."

I groan. "You're a scoundrel, sent to campus to seduce poor innocent men like me."

"Is it working?"

"Am I standing here breaking every single promise I'd ever made to myself?"

He unhooks the latch at my shoulder, letting my cape drop to the floor. "You're wearing too many clothes."

"I'll be the judge of that." I drag my fingers down his bare chest, reaching the first button done up over his abs. "I almost don't want these clothes off," I tell him. "You look dangerous like this."

"It's the sword, isn't it?"

"No." But it's cute he thinks that. "It's not knowing what I'm capable of with you around."

"Then why don't we find out?" He tilts his head up, lips hovering by mine. "Unless you're afraid."

"What do I have to be afraid of?" I'm not even thinking about my father or being outed. With Dash, it feels like nothing can touch us. He'd never tell my secret, so here, in my room, we're invincible.

"You might be richer than god and have a family legacy, but when our clothes come off, we're equals. It terrifies you, doesn't it? To know that body to body, there's no differences between us. You don't have status or riches to fall back on. I don't want you for any of those things. You have a cock and balls, sweet lips, big hands, and an ass I want to sink my teeth into. But I have all those things too. Here, with me, you're no one special. No one except the man I want to fuck."

"You're wrong."

"Oh, really?"

My gaze is stuck on his mouth as I drag my thumb across it. "There's nothing sweet about your lips."

"Might need to taste them again to be sure."

"What happened to me being in charge?"

He grunts, grabbing my lapels and flipping us so he has me pressed up against the wall instead. "You were taking too long."

9

Dash

HOLY FUCK, WHY IS THIS GUY SO ADDICTIVE?

Kissing Archie Levine is like getting the one thing I've been thirsting for, but instead of quenching that thirst, it turns me into a desert. The way his mouth is working against mine is addictive.

Every kiss, every touch, every traded heavy breath, all of it is creating a need I don't know how to manage.

His heavy cock is hard against my hip as my fingers make a frenzied path down the buttons on his jacket. The costume is hot but so inconvenient. How did they have quick, dirty fucks in ye olde times?

I growl as I get the jacket open and have a full shirt of buttons to go.

"God damn, Arch," I gasp, breaking our kiss. "It's like you don't *want* me to touch you."

I get the cocky frat boy smile of my dreams as he grabs my shirt and flips us again. Having him press me to the door like this is really doing it for me. "Actually … I was thinking that we leave our clothes on."

"Huh? That's not sexy."

He chuckles low and kisses along my jaw. "I can't think of anything sexier than your pants around your thighs while I screw you up against this door."

"Ah, so you think I'm going to let you fuck me, do you?"

Levine looks up at me through his thick lashes. "Pretty please?"

I groan because my dick gets hard over anything to do with him. Anything. If he's ready to take control, no longer holding back from what he wants and needs, I'm ready to let him.

"What if I don't swing that way?" I'm testing him because I'm an asshole and I want to.

His warm breath shivers over my lips. "Then I'm sure there are plenty of other fun things we can think of."

I smirk and reach for my pants. "Lucky for you, I don't think I'm capable of the word 'no' where you're concerned."

"Really?" Something lights up in his eyes. "What makes me such a special case?"

"Just call me a sucker for a sob story." I drop my pants and turn to face the door. "I'm ready when you are."

The touch I'm expecting doesn't come, and when I glance back over my shoulder at him, his stare is fixed on my ass, and while there's a hell of a lot of want there, he's obviously conflicted too.

"What's wrong?"

"I, uh, don't know …"

"What you're doing?" Damn, that's cute. "Grab your lube, and I'll talk you through it."

"You will?"

"I could do it myself, but it's hotter for me if you get my hole exactly the way your cock needs it."

He hisses and rubs his palm against the front of his pants.

"What's wrong? Gonna come before you're even inside me?"

"I need you to shut up now," he says, long strides getting him to his dresser that he rummages through until he produces the lube. He's got it open and coating his fingers on the way back to me. "I can't believe this is happening …"

"I often have that effect on men."

The unimpressed snort sounds like a bull ready to charge. Then his fingers slip into my crease, forearm hitting the wall beside mine, and body pressing against my side. He kisses the hinge of my jaw. "I want to be the best you've ever had."

"Ambitious of you."

His fingertip plays with my hole. "You'll soon learn that I don't settle for mediocrity."

"And yet you're planning on fucking me anyway."

His gravelly hum is right by my ear, and when he speaks, his deep tone floods me with warmth. "You are, hands down, the single most sexy, tempting man I've ever seen. I don't settle. I don't do things by halves. When my cock is inside you, I'll be fucking you knowing that I have the ultimate prize on my dick."

I shiver as his lips meet my neck. "Don't think I've ever been called a prize before. A cheap hole is common though."

His fingers leave my hole like he's been zapped, but before I can pretend I'm lying and tell him to go back to thinking I'm a catch, his hand comes down on my ass *hard.*

I yelp at the slap, sure he'll leave welts, cock throbbing over the intense pain.

"No more."

"What?" I ask, trying to get my vision straight after that intense sting.

"No more sleeping with men who don't know what they have with you. Like you said, together, like this, we're equals. People call me a king in this world." His raspy voice drops as his lips press against my ear. "So, if I tell you that you're gold standard, that's the only opinion that matters."

The cocky confidence has me grinning. Has me feel like I could fly. This is what I'd been hoping a hookup with him would be like—taking whatever he wants, full control and assertiveness. There are some men I like to play with and take control over, but when it comes to Archie Levine, his world-ending confidence is one of the things I took notice of first.

"Deal," I say, wanting to bring out more of his posses-siveness. "I'll make sure people tell me I have a gold-star hole before I let them fuck me."

He grunts. "After you've had me, no one else will compare."

"That so?" I turn my head so we're eye to eye. "Sounds like maybe I shouldn't let you, then. Since it's this one time and I'm going to be ruined and all."

He leans in, bites down on my bottom lip, and drags it through his teeth. His fingers reach down again, and this time, his finger meets my hole with more pressure.

"Push it in."

He does, and his eyes flutter as it sinks into my body. "I've just decided."

"What?"

"This hole is mine now."

I'm too slow to smother my moan.

"You like that?"

"Shit. Apparently."

"Do you like knowing that I haven't been able to get you out of my head? That when I jerk off, you're the only one I can think of? That I'm scared once I fuck you, that's all I'll ever want to be doing with my life?"

"It'd be hard to be a lawyer with your cock in my ass."

He shudders. "I don't care."

It's obvious he's only saying all this because he's horny and playing with an ass for the first time, but it's nice to pretend. Nice to think I could be the sole focus of a man like Archie. So, I'll play along and gladly indulge his fantasies, even when we both know that having a homophobic family isn't something you can just get past because you want a bit of sex.

Because I can't help myself, I ask, "What about your girlfriend?"

"There is no girlfriend."

"Good. Then hurry up and get another finger in me."

The first tiny crack in his confidence makes his forehead crease. "Now?"

"Yes."

"You sure?"

"I've been fucked enough that prep is usually fast. Except for a cock as fat as yours." Oh, look, there my mouth goes, trying to make him jealous again.

By the way his eyes darken, it's worked. "Stop talking about other men."

"There's only one way to get me to do that."

"Tell me."

"Do me so hard I forget all their names. I forget everyone except you."

He doesn't need to know that he's already given me that. Already made me hungry for him and only him.

Levine spears me on two fingers so suddenly there's a slight burn. He presses them deep, fills me to the knuckle, and strokes over my taint with the fingers resting against it. "How's that for learning?"

"Fuck me with them."

He does. Thrusting his fingers in and out until they're moving easier, he then adds a third. I rock back onto his hand, wanting and needing more. "Are you ready yet?"

"Yes. Put your dick in me."

He shifts like he's about to do it, and I laugh.

"Condom first."

"Really?"

"Unless you've had a recent health checkup you wanna whip out and show me, yes."

"Shit. Didn't even think of that." He pulls his fingers out, and my poor hole is left trying to clench onto nothing. He returns to rummaging through his drawer, and this time, he takes the crown off and tosses it before returning to me. Even with his jacket open and hair ruffled, he's an impressive sight. Especially when he reaches down and undoes his pants, pulling his cock out through the zipper.

My face floods with heat. Body feels too tight and

restrictive. I wasn't lying about him having a thick cock. Reddened and swollen, the tip glistens with precum.

My exhale is louder than I mean it to be. "I'll be honest with you," he says as he rolls the condom down his shaft. "All I want is to flood your hole with my cum. You make me act and feel not like myself. I haven't worked out if it's a good thing or not."

"My advice? Don't think about it. Just get inside me and fuck me like your life depends on it."

He presses against my back, heat wrapping around me and cock slotting into my crack. "I really think it might."

"Let's test that theory out, then."

Archie's lips press against the side of my neck as he reaches between us. The tip of his cock presses to my hole, and I sigh, relaxing into him as he presses forward.

"Holy fuck," he gasps, teeth scraping my skin. "Fuck. *Fuck*."

"Don't you dare come."

"It's your fault."

"How?"

"For feeling this good. My cock is in heaven."

"Actually, I'm Dash, not heaven, but guys make that mistake a lot."

He slams home with a grunt. "What did I say about mentioning others?"

"What did I say about making me forget?"

Archie's fingers bite into my hips as he straightens and slams into me, over and over, like a man on a mission.

Joke's on him though, because I've already forgotten. All I can think of is his presence, the way he's filling me, stretching my ass so wide it almost hurts, but every thrust has him passing over my prostate and making me see stars.

The music from the party is still pounding through the house, people shrieking and stumbling past in the hall outside, with no idea that I'm being fucked within an inch of my life on the other side of this door. I'll admit that it's a turn-on knowing Archie is the one behind me. That the prized Kappa frat boy chose to stick his dick in me, out of everyone at the party. I'm not getting all swoony over being chosen because I know how fickle men can be, and I'm not kidding myself into thinking it's more than it is— I've dealt with closeted guys enough to know how it all ends—but for this one single moment in time, he chose me, and I get to ride that high of being better than everyone else.

Fucked-up? Why, thank you, I am.

But when you're an average kid from an average family on a scholarship and working your ass off to get ahead, getting to be picked, to have attention, to be the one guy to catch Levine's eye … yeah, that's doing things to my dick I'd never admit out loud.

"How about now?" he grits through his teeth. "What are you thinking about now?"

Feeling evil, I say, "How this is maybe the third hardest fuck I've ever had."

His grip tightens, nails digging into my skin. "I'm going to wreck you."

"Less promising, more doing."

I'm struggling to stay upright he's fucking me so hard though. I'm pushing back into every thrust, loving the millisecond pause as he drives as deep as he can go before pulling back and slamming in again. Archie's clearly not a virgin, but I'm getting the impression he's been every bit as desperate for this as I've been. He fucks me like a man possessed, like he's lost control over his body and is being driven by pure need.

Each thrust sends me into the wall, lighting up all the nerves in my ass, and the hem of my shirt is brushing the tip of my oversensitive cock in a way that's driving me wild.

Archie's panting heavily by my ear, and this weird moment slips over me where reality shifts and we're no longer in a frat house or on campus or … anywhere.

White noise fills my mind, and all I'm aware of is the man behind me and the way he's promised to ruin me and has.

"I can't hold out much longer," he warns, smashing through the high.

"Then do it. Let go." I use his fantasy against him. "Fill me with your cum, Archie. Mark my hole as yours."

"Oh, fuck." He slips off rhythm, thrusts shorter and wilder as he pounds his way to the end. He cries out as he comes, random curses and mutters slipping from his lips before he slows and finally stills.

As soon as he sinks against my back, cock still buried inside me, I take his hand from my hip and wrap it around my dick.

He immediately strokes me, long and smooth, smearing precum over my length as the sound of him catching his breath hits my ear. He presses his hips tighter to my ass, speeding up his hand as he gains his confidence and sends my legs to jelly. His free hand wraps around me, and I'm torn between whether he's holding me up or I'm standing on my own.

I squeeze my ass around him as my balls tighten, feeling so full and filthy and fucking horny. I'm riding the edge. Ready for Archie to send me over it. The arm across my chest makes me feel trapped, and I'm surprised by how much I like it. Him, holding me there while he gets me off because he wants to get me off.

An electric charge builds at the base of my spine as I drop my head back against his shoulder, orgasm building and building until it's too strong to hold back.

Then, Archie drags his tongue up my neck, and when he reaches my ear, he says, "Say my name."

The pressure releases. Cum floods his fists, and through the rush of brain-fogging endorphins, I force it out. "Archie. Fuck, *Archie* …"

His cum-covered hand grasps my jaw and jerks my head toward him. The kiss is possessive and wild, and I meet his madness with more of my own. My orgasm might have been receding, but the way I want him has only gotten worse, and my whole body aches with how much I need this to happen again.

No man has ever had this effect over me before.

I press all my frustrations into the kiss and tell that stupid little voice to fuck off.

10

Archie

I stay inside Dash for as long as humanly possible, but now that I've come, my cock can only do so much. I soften inside him, and no matter how I try to fight it, I slip out anyway.

He groans and breaks the kiss, leaning forward to press his forehead to the door. His ribs expand heavily as he tries to catch his breath. "Just gimme a moment to recover, and I'll go."

Go? I step away, pulling the condom off and tossing it into my trash can. From this angle, I have a perfect view of Dash's abused hole, and all I can think is how I want to be back inside there again. Now. Tomorrow. All weekend.

My brain is all mushy after what happened. There's no way to describe how sex with Dash has changed my whole life, and every time I try to find words to explain, they feel empty and meaningless.

I've always been powerful. Always had a powerful position in life. But for the first time ever, I felt it. Felt power beyond anything money or notoriety can give.

Dash giving me control over his body like that was the first time I actually felt in control of myself as well. The first time, ever, that I felt like me.

And so, despite the warnings going off in my head about Father and gossip and whatever the hell else, I say exactly what I want to say and fuck the consequences.

"I don't want you to go."

Dash whips around to look at me. "What?"

I cross back over to him, and with only the slightest hesitation, I turn him and reach for the buttons on his shirt. "I said I want you to stay. With me. In my bed. Where I can fill your greedy hole whenever I get hard and touch you in all the moments in between."

His dark eyes study me, perfectly bowed lips stark red against his pale skin and slightly swollen from our kisses. I love looking at him and knowing I did that. Love that Dash's usual bravado is dimmed by curiosity.

I open the first button, both of us watching the other. Then I move on to the next one.

"And what if someone sees?" he asks, voice low.

"I don't owe anyone an explanation."

"You're a Levine."

"I'm in college. Experimenting is an unspoken rule."

Dash cocks his head, messy black hair shifting and a glimmer of that snark coming alive in his face. "Is that what this is? Experimenting?"

I shake my head because experimenting implies that I don't already know what I want. "This is me taking what I want while I still have time to do it."

"And I'm what you want," he taunts.

He can joke all he likes, but he has no idea how true those words are. I finish unbuttoning his shirt and spread it open, taking in his gorgeous, masculine body. He's skinnier than I am, lightly muscled, with deep depressions running either side of his hips down toward where his cock is hanging soft from a bed of dark pubes.

My breath punches in my lungs at the sight of him.

"Get rid of your pants."

He kicks off his shoes and finishes shucking his pants while I shrug out of my jacket and undo my shirt. He watches me undress, shamelessly checking me out, and I can't ever remember enjoying revealing each part of me for someone.

When we're naked, I grab his hip, covered in red marks from my hands, and tug him toward my bed.

"Did I hurt you?" I ask as I climb in, then hold the covers up for him.

"Yep." He sucks his bottom lip into his mouth before releasing it again. "Loved it though."

"You loved when I hit your ass too."

He rolls onto his side to face me. I stay lying on my back, trying to get my heart to settle over the fact that I'm lying in bed with another man. With Dash.

"Apparently, I like it when you get rough with me."

"What? You've never liked it with other guys?"

"Ah, now who's bringing them up?" His eyes shine with amusement. "But since you asked, no. There's not a lot of guys I'll let do whatever they want."

I hate how much I love hearing that. "There you go making me feel special again."

"I'm not sure special is the right word for it."

I hook an eyebrow upward and roll up onto my side, and then I reach around to slip a finger into his used hole. "Clearly, not all of you agrees with that."

He grins and runs a hand over my chest. "Fine. You won. Succeeded. Ruined me for all men."

The nerves in my gut go wild, and that possessive streak finally settles. I leave his ass and run my hand up his smooth back instead, shocked by the notion that I'm, that we're … what? Cuddling?

"What's that look?" Dash asks.

I debate whether to be honest or not, but fuck it. What do I have to lose? "Am I allowed to admit this is really fucking nice?"

"What? Having a ready hole on hand?"

I scowl, pissed that he can't be serious for a second. "Forget it."

"Ooh, that made you mad."

"What did you think it was going to do? I'm lying here thinking how great it feels to be here, talking and holding you like this, and you think I—whatever, Dash. I don't give a shit."

I flop onto my back, not liking the way my chest hurts.

Silence wraps around us. It stretches so thin the pressure in the room increases.

Dash shifts closer, pauses, then lies down, finding a place for his head on my shoulder. "I'm sorry."

"Right. Okay."

"I guess I've never thought about snuggling before."

I scowl. "We're not snuggling."

He wraps his arm around my waist. "Oh, yeah? How about now?"

Smart-ass. I can hear in his voice that he's amused, but fuck him. This feels too good anyway. Instead of shoving him off, I wrap both arms around him and pull him tighter against me, skin to skin, feeling heated and so damn good.

"This is snuggling, asshole."

He tries to stifle his laugh in my shoulder but fails. "As I was saying. I don't really do this."

"You don't?"

"Nah, I mean, once sex is over, I don't see much point in sticking around."

"So why did you tonight?"

"Easy. You promised me more."

I don't like that answer, but what else was I expecting?

"You're saying that if I want this again, all I have to do is promise you sex?"

"Exactly." His fingers trace patterns across my abs and up to my chest. "I was thinking I could ride you next time."

"Yeah? Works for me because I was thinking I'd like to try sucking you off."

"I'm so down for that."

I almost roll my eyes. "Shocking. Really. What a surprise."

"Sue me. I like sex."

"Maybe I shouldn't say this, but … I've never seen sex as something to like."

"What do you mean?"

I don't know what Dash and I are to each other, but I do know that I want to feel understood, and he's the only person I can talk to about this. "It's always been an obligation. Get hard, get it in, get it over with."

His fingers pause.

"You …" I swallow, not wanting to get emotional over this. "I don't think you'll ever understand how different it is with you."

"No, I get it."

"Do you?"

"Not totally, but I know what you're saying. Know what it was like the first time I had sex with a man after wanting it for so long. The way it's not even completely about the sex and partially just about feeling like you know who you are now."

"Yes. That's … it's exactly it."

Dash lifts his head, and when he looks at me, there's a softness to it I'm not expecting. "Kinda love I got to be the one to give you that."

I kiss him because he's here and I want to, and maybe because I don't want to speak right now in case my voice does something stupid as I get the words out. "Thank you."

"The thing is …"

"Yeah?"

"I'm thinking. And, well, it seems to me like you have to be super far into the closet, right?"

Some of my good mood shifts. "Yup."

"Well, you know … I'm here."

"Okay …"

"I mean, that if you want someone to keep letting off steam with … like, you officially ruined me for other men, so, it's like, might as well keep going until the whole newness of you wears off, right? And it's not like you can have sex with anyone else, so if you wanted—"

My laugh is more relief than anything. "You wanna be my fuck buddy?"

"I'm just saying it's on the table."

It's a struggle to stop from immediately accepting and giving away how eager I am for that. I push up his bandana, buying myself more time as I fling it across the room and try to flatten his wild hair. It's long enough to tuck some behind his ear, and I do it slowly, loving how natural it feels with him.

"No one else."

"What?"

I'm not sure if he doesn't understand me or doesn't like my question, but it's a nonnegotiable for me.

I roll on top of Dash, flattening him into my mattress. "I don't want anyone else touching you. I *can't* have anyone else touching you. The thought that you were in the bushes with some other guy earlier is making me see red when—"

Dash cuts me off. "Arch, I was making you jealous. He's my roommate, and when you saw us, we were sneaking in, not hooking up."

"What?"

The asshole looks way too amused. "I love how jealous you get. Want me to be all yours, huh? Your dick? Your hole?"

"My lips, my jaw, my throat, my nipples, my abs. Mine." I grip him tighter. "I've never been good with sharing."

"I'm not looking for a relationship."

"Your choice." Disappointment roars in my ears. "But knowing you were with some other man would eat at me. Every time I thought about you over the last weeks, all I could picture was you kissing that man in the hallway, and it made me want to punch something."

"Anyone ever told you that you're intense?"

"Never." The way I'm behaving isn't how I've ever been before. Lizzie could have been sleeping with all the guys on campus, and I wouldn't have cared, but Dash? I need him to be mine. "Don't walk away from me," I whisper.

Dash smiles. "Oh, I have no plans to. I just wanted to push and see how serious you were."

"I … I can't come out," I remind him.

"No, I know. That was my whole reason for the suggestion." He leans up to kiss me, slowly, teasingly. My cock is already hard from this conversation, and that only makes the situation worse. "You can fuck me whenever you want to fuck me," he says, reaching for my drawer and pulling out a condom. "And I can fuck you whenever I want to fuck you. We'll be each other's stress relief." He tears the condom open with his teeth and reaches down to roll it over my cock. Then, he parts his legs and guides me to his hole, pressing my tip to it before I take over and sink in deep. It's a blinding relief to be back inside him. "This is yours now," he continues, voice a little deeper. "Whenever you need it. Take it. Just you. And when we're done …" He kisses me again. "I'll let you snuggle me all you like. No boyfriends. No obligations. I need you as much as you need me."

I melt against him, hearing everything I need to hear. Our mouths fuse as we move together, no hurry this time, joined together with mutual need as I rock inside him until I come.

The party goes on until the early hours, and we're awake even longer. Fast sex, lazy sex, using our hands and mouths and my cock in his ass.

When daybreak hits and Dash assures me it's time for him to go, I have to hold back from begging him to stay. I could survive all day like this. All week, hell, maybe all month.

Just him and me. Talking and sex.

I'm exhausted, but my mind has never been more alive.

He slips out the door, and I can't shake the feeling everything has changed. For good.

11

Dash

BEING WITH ARCHIE IS HOT ENOUGH IN ITSELF, BUT THE sneaking around aspect is thrilling. I'm like double dick seven, agent of sexpionage, swooping in to make sure his every need is met.

And fuck me, I've never had this much sex in my life. Archie is a horny guy, and he's constantly blowing up my phone, asking me to meet, and whisking me away to secluded spots on campus for a quickie.

Then at night, if Larry is out, he'll come by my place, or I'll sneak into the Kappa house.

Our arrangement is my new favorite thing. Who needs schoolwork and friendships and part-time jobs? Not me.

Unfortunately, those things get in the way of us constantly being together, along with Archie's frat duties, but we're making it work.

"Excuse me."

I jump at the voice, cutting through the stillness of the library, and find Archie leaning against the nearest stacks.

"Hey," Jonah from my study group says. "Need something?"

"Do you care if I steal Dash away for a few minutes?"

Jonah shakes his head, and I have to force myself to get up calmly instead of jumping on Archie and fusing our faces together.

"What's up?"

Archie nods toward the next row, and I follow him there. The second we're hidden from view, his warm hand slips into mine, and he picks up the pace, dragging me along behind him. We go from row to row, moving into the quieter, more secluded areas of the stacks until we reach the back corner where the paleontology books are. He presses me into the shelves, and before I can think to ask what the hell he's doing, he kisses me.

Archie's lips aren't like anyone's I've ever kissed before. The man is skilled, and I hate how quickly I lose all common sense when he's around. Like now, when I should be worried about us being busted, but all I do is wind my fingers through his hair and kiss him harder.

Archie pulls back, laughing against my lips. "You're almost as eager as I am."

"No almost about it. Do you cover your lips with crack before you see me? Fucking hell."

"I don't, but that's an idea." He presses one more soft kiss to my lips, then steps back until he's leaning against the books opposite me. "Hey."

"I think the option for greetings ended around the time you were tonguing my tonsils."

He snickers. "Even my tongue isn't that good."

"Probably doesn't help that I don't *have* tonsils."

Archie's bluey-green eyes crease at the corners as he smiles at me. The look is soft and sends my gut awash. "Did you have them out when you were little?"

"Yeah, I used to get tonsilitis a lot. So …" I make a slashing motion over my throat.

"Me too."

"Really?"

"Look at that. Something we have in common."

"There was bound to be something." I kick the toe of his shoe. "What did you hunt me down for? I need to study, but if you're after a hookup, Larry works tonight, so you can meet me later."

Archie's gaze drops to his feet. "I … Actually, I don't really know."

"You hunted me down in the library with no clue why?"

He scowls. "I was already *in* here and spotted you. I don't even remember deciding to come over, actually. One minute, I was by the doors; the next, I was fetching you. So, uh, sorry."

"Don't be. I love being so wanted it's not even a conscious decision anymore."

"Well, it would be nice to know what that feels like," he teases.

"Please. I've always been so frustratingly into you with no reason to be other than your pretty face."

"And now?"

I tilt my head from side to side. "There's kinda a personality under there."

"Hey, fuck you."

"You do. Frequently."

His cheeks flush, and he glances both ways down the stacks. "Come on a date with me."

"What?"

"It'll be fun."

"What part of 'not boyfriends' did you miss?"

"The part where apparently that somehow means we can't hang out together."

Do I want to hang out with him? Of course, but I also know it's probably not the smartest thing to be seen around campus together. "There's literally no reason for us to be seen together. We're not friends."

"Well, maybe we are now."

"Oh yeah?" I taunt. "Are you going to go around introducing me as your new bestie?"

A muscle in Archie's jaw pulses.

"Exactly. If we're seen together too much, people might start thinking there's something going on. We both know you can't afford for that to happen."

His face pulls so tight I swear he's ready to kick something. "There's no reason why we can't be friends. I want to be friends."

"Dude, relax. We *are* friends. No one else has to know that though. Don't worry about me—I'm not the kind of guy who needs romance and attention because I'm where you park your cock at night."

"Stop talking like that."

"Like *what*?"

"You … you …" His face is going redder. "Sometimes you make it sound so cheap. Stop fucking doing that."

I laugh, caught off guard by that twisted view. "What do you think this is? Sure, it's not cheap and nasty, but it's just sex. Incredible sex. We're friendly, I like talking to you, but damn, boy, we don't need to pretend this is anything more than it is."

"Maybe I want to pretend." He closes the distance between us, stopping before we touch. "Maybe I want to get swept up in having a crush and wrap myself in the illusion of a real relationship. I know it will never be anything, but maybe I don't want to deal with reality when I'm with you. Maybe I want to pretend like you're my boyfriend and we have a future, and I know how stupid that sounds, but why the fuck can't I be stupid for once?"

My jaw is somewhere around my ankles. "You don't know what you're saying."

"I know exactly what I'm saying."

My lips twitch as I hold back an inappropriate laugh. "You want to pretend to be boyfriends, knowing we're not actually boyfriends, so, that, what? When you have to fall in line and go back to being the straight boy, you think it'll be easier?"

Archie shakes his head, reddish curls swaying. "Oh no. Definitely not. It'll make it a thousand times harder."

My laugh breaks free. "Then what the heck are you talking about?"

He sets his hands on my hips. "If this is my one chance to experience the life I'm supposed to be living, I want to experience it. All of it. Obviously, there's a lot we can't do, but …" His voice breaks, and all my amusement shrivels up.

"It's not fair," I say.

"Don't I know it?"

There are no other words I can put it into, though, because he's probably already told himself it all. This is scummy. Fucked-up. His daddy doesn't want a gay son, so he gets what he wants? What about what Archie wants?

The problem with that question is that I don't know *what* he wants. Not really.

I'm safe for him. Convenient.

If he had the option to be out and free, I've gotta face the facts that I'd never be his guy. Can't say that doesn't hurt to acknowledge, but maybe this is the chance for both of us. He gets to fool himself into thinking he has a boyfriend, and I get to fool myself into thinking I could own a guy like Archie Levine.

"Deal."

He blinks at me. "What is?"

"We'll do it. Play your little game. Pretend boyfriends or whatever—not like it changes a whole lot. We're together whenever we can be anyway."

"Except now you'll let me take you on dates." His eyes search mine, and I sigh.

"Sure. That." Playing it off means I don't have to face how much I like that idea. "Just make sure it's somewhere expensive. Preferably with a five-week wait list."

"I don't think anything like that exists in this town."

"Fine …" I hook my finger through a gap between his buttons. "Guess burger and fries it is."

"Why don't you let me do the thinking?"

His amused tone lights me up inside. "Oh yeah? You gonna make me feel special? Wine and dine me before you sixty-nine me."

Archie's lips tighten briefly. "There you go making it sound cheap again."

"Cheap?" I can't believe *this* is the guy I'm into. "That sounds like the perfect romantic night to me."

"In that case, I'm taking notes."

"And now I'm legitimately excited about the idea of a date." I frown, wanting to be real for a moment but lost as to how to start. "You sure about this? I get all the reasons why you think it's a good idea, but I want to make sure you don't think it's something I need. It's not. I'm cool with our arrangement. You're ridiculously hot and eager for me—what's not to love?"

His answer shocks me. "No. I'm not sure at all. It's terrifying to think about my dad finding out or someone seeing us together or you telling people—"

"I wouldn't—"

"I know that, but they're all the thoughts constantly in my head. We wouldn't be here now if I didn't trust you. But it's because I'm scared that I know it's right. I'm so used to things being easy. I'm so used to money opening doors or my last name having people fall over themselves for me. This is the first locked door I've ever had in my life. And *I* opened it. Me. On my own. It's my choice to be here, and honestly, Dash, the more time I spend with you ... I'm so glad you took that chance on me. That's all. So no, I'm not sure. But that isn't going to stop me anyway."

"Well, that logic is good enough for me." I kiss him again, little sparks going off in my chest as his eyes go all crinkly and happy. "I've gotta get back to the others."

"Ah. Yeah. We've been a while."

"I'll just tell them I was helping a dumb jock with the Dewey decimal system."

"The sad part is that I can't even be offended by that.

Some of my brothers don't even know where the library is."

We slowly part from each other, hands lingering like we don't want to let go.

"Text me when you want to meet up," I tell him.

Archie watches me leave, and I've barely turned the corner to the study carrels when my phone vibrates in my pocket.

I already know it's him before I've ever pulled it and I find one message there waiting for me.

2nyt. Wear sumthing pretty 4 me.

12

Archie

PLANNING A DATE ON SHORT NOTICE ISN'T EASY, especially since I can't exactly take him out to a restaurant. I'm determined to make this good though, and I've got about an hour to do it.

We'll definitely finish up on that sixty-nine he wants, but it's the part between now and then that has me sweating.

"You good, Levine?" Steve asks, trying to see over my shoulder.

I shove him away, focusing back on my notepad and the complete lack of ideas on the paper. "Trying to plan a date."

"Oooh, Lizzie is a lucky lady."

I *hmph*, wishing it was easy enough to tell the truth. To say, "I'm gay, bro" and have the moment mean nothing to anyone. Instead, I'm too focused on the risk factor than finding a date idea that makes the guy I like feel sort of special. Dash … fuck, when I see him, it's like everything else doesn't exist. He tries to hide that vulnerability, that softness, behind snark and an uncaring attitude, but I see it.

Like he sees me.

We've only been fucking around for a couple of weeks, but I like him more than anyone I've ever met. I only wish it was easy enough to show him that, but I'm scared that no matter what I do, it will all fall flat.

"So, what are you thinking?" Steve asks, taking a seat at the dining table next to me. "Roses and dinner? Shopping? Any bands playing?"

"Bands?"

He shrugs. "Chicks like music, right?"

Everyone likes music. Including Dash, who always has something playing. I'm not up to date on bands or music styles, but I'll bet he is, and I'll bet he's a picky bastard.

I call Jameson, our president and the man who knows everything about everything.

"Hey, man, I have a question for you," I say as soon as he picks up. "Any chance you've heard about bands or events or anything on tonight?"

"Hold up, I'll run over and check the message board. I saw some flyers the other day for something."

I wait, glad I caught him while he was still on campus. Sitting across from Dash and getting a chance to chat would have been great, but hey, if it's somewhere dark where everyone is focused on a band, maybe dancing together is something we could make happen. I rub at the ache behind my sternum, both loving and hating the feeling.

My suggestion to Dash tonight was a stupid one because I know all that's coming for me is heartbreak, but I want to know what it's like. Just once. And Dash, with his beautiful smiles and vulnerable eyes and snarky mouth, will be the one to do it.

"You there?" Jameson asks.

"Sure am."

"There's some kind of punk rock band playing tonight at Bally's House. Nine p.m."

"That'll do. Thanks, brother."

"See you around."

He hangs up, and I immediately text Dash.

I'll grab u at 9. I no I said to dress pretty but make that sexy instead.

Dash:

Suspenders & thong it is

I laugh and head upstairs to change. Bands in a downtown basement aren't exactly my thing, but I'll make it work. Surely, I've got some cutoffs and a tank top here somewhere.

Apparently not, and I end up having to raid Steve's clothes, but by the time I leave to pick up Dash, I'm feeling good about things. My arms are out, the hundred push-ups I did before I left have them looking good, and the mix of nerves and excitement in my gut can't even be settled by the image of what Father would say if he could see me.

The only thing that matters is Dash.

Except when he climbs into my car—wearing suspenders over his tank top and that bandana back in his hair—he eyes me, looking torn between horror and amusement.

"Slumming it, are we?"

I grin bashfully and back the car out of the drive. "Not impressed by my outfit choice?"

"Actually, I don't think I've ever been more attracted to you in my life. Here I thought I was only after you for your money."

Even though that's been a concern of mine basically my entire life, there's nothing about Dash that makes me believe it's true. He doesn't care about money or things. He's working toward his own future, and he knows that won't be with me.

My lack of response must worry him.

"That was a joke, by the way," he says. "We both know you're after *me* for *my* money."

I snort. "Oh, yes. Expanding my wealth is top of my priorities."

"Isn't it always for rich, white dudes?"

I pinch his thigh, and he cries out, rubbing the spot, then retaliates by twisting my nipple.

"Ah! Driving!"

"Don't start what you can't finish, Levine."

"I have no problems finishing, which you know well."

"One of my favorite things about you."

I drag my bottom lip through my teeth as I wonder whether to ask what I want to. Fuck it. "What else do you like?"

"Your dick."

I should have seen that coming. "Okay, what about me do you like that doesn't involve sex?"

A silence creeps in after my words.

"Wow. *Ouch.*"

"Well, what do you like about me?" he fires back.

Even though I asked first, apparently, I'm not as afraid of my emotions as he is. "You're trustworthy. You're fun. You like to live in the moment. You love your family, and you know you need to work hard in life and actually want to earn everything you achieve."

"Huh." Dash swallows, and I glance over in time to see his Adam's apple bob. "So that's … things."

"We talk a lot."

"You remember a lot."

"About you."

He shifts in his seat. "I didn't realize you were paying all that much attention. I mean, how do you focus after sex?"

He still hasn't answered my question, and I try to ignore how shitty that makes me feel. The bitterness in my voice isn't as easy to hide. "When you like someone, you sort of care about what they have to say."

He still doesn't answer, and we pull up at Bally's House without talking again. I could linger on the thought that Dash is only here for the sex, or I could go back to the land of delusions and forget that reality exists.

So that's what I do.

As soon as we park, I lean over the center console and pull him into a toe-curling kiss. "Hey."

His expression is dopey when I pull back. "Now, that's a greeting." He glances out the windscreen. "Where are we?"

"There's a band playing. Thought we could join the mosh pits and head banging."

Dash bursts out laughing as we climb from the car. "Is it a metal band?"

"What's metal?"

"Oh, sweet Jesus. Just follow me and try not to open your mouth."

I duck my mouth by his ear. "Then how will I suck you off later?"

He groans and takes my hand to tug me through the door.

We let go almost instantly, and I follow him down the rickety metal stairs into the basement area of the club. It's a smaller room, with a bar along one wall and a low stage up the back.

I don't know what I was expecting, but the lighting is terrible, the crowd is thick, and I'm worried if I touch something, I'll contract a disease.

Disappointment crashes through me.

"Fuck. I am so, so sorry."

When Dash turns to me, his eyes have lit up. "About what?"

I gesture to the stuffy, humid room. "This wasn't what I had in mind."

"This is perfect!"

"It is?"

Dash is almost bouncing as he takes my hand again. His hair and eyes look dark against his pale skin in the dim lighting. "This band is good—not metal—and look around at the crowd. They skew older. No college people. No one to recognize us. You wanted boyfriends, let's be boyfriends."

I cast my eyes over the crowd, wondering if we can be open here. Out. There's so, so much that can go wrong.

"What if … *somebody* doesn't like it?"

"We're not going to be humping on the dance floor. We'll still be discreet."

My hope is hesitant, but I can't hold it back. "Okay."

"Let's go."

The band is already partway through a number as we push our way into the crowd. Dash looks at home here, like he's somewhere he belongs, and that fills me with the confidence to shadow him through the dancing bodies until we're surrounded on all sides. The flashes of the colored stage lighting are all that's brightening the space, and here, cocooned by bodies and sweat, music so loud it's beating in my eardrums, I feel safe.

Safe enough to pull Dash in front of me and put my hands on his hips.

We're not standing super close, we're not touching anywhere else, but there's so much chaos around us that no one is paying attention to two stray guys touching in the dark.

Dash dances like he was born into this madness, and I try to keep up. It doesn't take long for me to get hot and sweaty, zoned out to everything but the music and the beautiful man in my grip.

His head falls back, messy hair brushing my bare shoulder, and gives me a smile that lights me up from my toes to my scalp. The smile is completely free, and in this moment, it's created for me and me alone.

The crowd gets thicker as the night goes on, Dash and I pressed together no matter how much I try to fight it. His ass ends up in my crotch, and every movement brushes against me in a way that has me rock hard by the band's final number.

I duck down to his ear and shout to be heard over the music. "Let's go before everyone else does."

"Okay, grandpa."

I rub my hard dick against his ass cheek. "This is more of an impatience thing."

Dash gets the message, grin wicked and hand in mine as he pushes his way back through the crowd again.

The whole time he's leading us out, I follow.

The ache in my chest tells me I'd follow him anywhere.

13

Dash

ARCHIE IS ACTING WEIRD. HE DOESN'T EVEN LOOK around as he backs me inside my apartment, barely breaking the kiss to slam the door closed behind us.

Tonight has been fun, and even though I like to pretend the whole boyfriend game is a dumb idea, I didn't hate it. Knowing Archie is mine, at least temporarily, is giving me the kinds of vibes I've never had before.

His question from earlier is still swirling in my head as well. It was easy enough to put it off while we were fucking around to the music, but now it's getting loud again. A solid reminder that I need to face that maybe I'm growing feelings here, and he wants me to put those feelings into words.

Words have never been my strong point. Not when it comes to talking about emotion. I get that it's healthy, and guys are encouraged to do that, but it doesn't make it any easier.

Except for Archie. He doesn't seem to have an issue when it comes to laying it all out there and making me sweat.

"How did you want to end the night again?" he asks.

It takes me a moment to follow. "Sixty-nine?"

"I'm game if you are."

Holy hell am I game, but … "I'm all sweaty."

"And?"

"Trust me when I say that sweaty dick is *not* a delicacy."

Archie snorts a laugh, sweet eyes creasing. "So …"

"Shower first?"

He nods quickly. "Yeah. That."

We tumble into my tiny bathroom, and I lock the door before switching the shower to hot. Archie strips off, and I take a moment to watch him reveal all that sexy fucking skin. His broad shoulders and trim waist wake my dick as I shamelessly eye-fuck him.

"Careful," he warns, eyes darkening. "We can't do what you want to do in the shower, and if you keep looking at me like that, I'm going to have you against the wall, making me come in the next minute."

I run my fingertips down his heated skin, loving the way goose bumps prickle to life after them. He catches my hand before I can reach his dick and lifts it to his lips.

"You're perfect, Dash." His voice is husky, hair frizzly from the steam. I make the mistake of meeting his eyes, and I swear there'll never be a day where I don't get lost in them.

"Me? Fucking hell, Levine, I don't think I've ever met a guy like you before. You're so … like, warm, I guess. When you want something, you go for it, but not in an obnoxious way. Ever since that first time we spoke, you've made me feel like a someone, like there's something important about me, and I don't think I've ever had that. Ever. You're a good person, and I can't remember the last time I met a legitimately good person, but it's not all bullshit with you. You have everything, but you don't act like you do." I hang my head, wishing I could stop talking but not able to make myself. "You asked what I like about you, and I couldn't answer because I like everything. It sounds dumb as fuck to say, but the day this ends, it's going to be really goddamn hard because I've never met a single other person like you in my life."

Archie's fingers find my chin and tilt my head upward, and before I can look at him, his mouth crashes with mine. We end up under the steam of the shower, not caring that the water is hot enough to melt our skin because there's nothing more important to me, right now, than kissing him.

Every kiss is given like it's the last time, and I both love and hate the feeling. Archie doesn't break from me as he flicks open my bodywash and pours it over us both. The soapy liquid makes exploring his skin easier, and I take my time mapping and washing his muscles, committing every soft plane to memory.

I'm so hard. My dick is trapped between us, flush against his, slick with water, bodywash, and precum. Archie sighs into my mouth and palms my balls, and I'm sure he can feel how erratic my heartbeat is with my chest pressed against his.

"I think we're clean," he mutters.

I drag my tongue up his neck, tasting water and chemical, stopping as I reach his earlobe. "Confirmed. You taste delicious."

He flicks off the water. "My cum tastes even better."

"I know. I've become familiar with the taste of your cum lately."

We both grab a towel, and I greedily watch as he wraps it around his hips, then clicks open the door and peers out.

"Don't think anyone's home."

"Good. Get that sexy ass into my bed."

He tosses me a heart-stopping grin before ducking into the hall, and I reach down to adjust myself before I follow him. By the time I get to my room, he's standing beside my bed, completely naked, dragging the towel over his hair.

I wolf whistle, and Archie goes a gorgeous shade of red.

"How do we do this?"

"You've never sixty-nined before?"

"Not with a cock ramming my tonsils."

I smirk. "Ah, but we already established you don't have any of those."

Before I can tell him to get on his back, he grabs my hip and reels me in toward him. Archie kisses my nose, and it's possibly the sweetest, softest moment of my life.

"I know I'm about to do some very filthy things to you, but I want you to know that I value you first."

Urg, too cute. I push him onto the bed. "Respect is overrated. Use me like your little whore."

"You want that?"

"I want everything from you." I climb up beside him, hair dripping on the sheets, and press a quick kiss to his lips. "Including your mouth around my dick. You ready for it?"

Archie looks so sweetly eager my balls ache.

Instead of focusing on how this damn man makes me feel, I flip around and drop onto my side. Then I roll Archie onto his until his dick is hovering right in front of my face. My cock throbs at the sight of him, all thick and swollen, smooth head and prominent vein. He's a work of porny art, and I stick out my tongue to lap at his slit because I can't hold back anymore.

Archie's groan simmers in my gut.

He closes his mouth over me, the warmth, the wetness, the soft sucking … it rearranges my brain. Archie Levine might be a baby gay, but he's a quick study. He's gone from zero cock-sucking skills to taking my cock like a champ, and if we get nothing else out of this relationship, I'll be glad to have at least given him a skill he'll use for life.

Or, on the times the straightness becomes too much, and he snaps before darting back in the closet.

It hurts me to think of that future for him. The struggle with who he is and what it'll do to him. I try to ignore it, push it out, focus on giving him head and making it the best it can be. But no matter how good things are with him, how much I love spending time with him and making him come, it always holds that tinge of bitterness. Archie deserves the world, and all he's going to end up with is emptiness.

I'm obsessed with his taste, love the way his thick weight feels on my tongue. Nothing turns me on more than having my jaw stretched around him, knowing I'm giving him the same intense pleasure he's bringing out in me.

My balls are aching with their load as he sucks me. Archie's great at a sloppy blow job, and those are my favorite kinds. The way spit covers his chin and my balls, the way my dick rams at his throat, the way his breathing gets heavier and more desperate, like he's too invested in sucking me off than breathing.

I pull off him briefly to get my fingers nice and wet, and then I reach around and play with his ass. His sudden inhale has me freezing, but then he doubles down on my shaft, and I have the green light to keep going.

His head bobs up and down faster, while I run my tongue over every ridge I can fit in my mouth. My fingertips circle his opening, lightly stroking the sensitive skin as I get him used to the feel of me down there. I have no idea if he'd ever let me fuck him, but we've talked about it being a possibility. One day. Like we have all the time in the world.

I squeeze my eyes closed at the thought. It doesn't matter what I do though; I can't push the ever-present memory of our end date from my mind. That's the fucked-up part about what we're doing—we're both taking what we want, pretending we get to have it all, knowing that one day, probably soon, it's going to wreck us.

My feelings for him have been manageable so far, but every day we spend together, every text, every call, every stolen moment is messing with my head. The broken shards behind my sternum keep poking at my heart, and I do my best to ignore them, but there are times, times like now, where the pain is overwhelming.

I thrust into Archie's mouth, wanting to selfishly take everything I can from him while I have that option. I give him the same. Show him through the way I suck and lick, through the way I play with his hole, that there's nowhere I'd want to be than right here.

Than with him.

My orgasm is creeping up on me. Archie's hips buck, and it makes me think he's in a similar state. Rocketing closer to release, ready to fall into the high I'm craving. My balls are tight, cock aching, and all it takes is his fingers slipping behind my balls to the sensitive skin behind them for me to finally let go.

I pulse into his mouth, riding the crest of my orgasm. It takes a few seconds more for him to follow me, and he floods my mouth with his cum.

I greedily drink it all down, not wanting to stop, not wanting to crash from the sex because the second we part, Archie will either be too sweet for me to handle, or he'll want to talk, and both of those things are ones I want to put off as long as possible.

He pulls off me, forehead dropping to rest on my thigh. His chest is moving deeply with every breath, and I hit that point where I have to let him out of my mouth, too, or risk shit getting weird.

I release him and roll onto my back.

Archie immediately flips around and lowers his body onto mine. Fuck, I hate how much I love having him there.

His eyes are soft as he leans down and drags a slow kiss over my lips. "I wish I could keep you," he whispers.

I wish I could keep him too.

14

Archie

WHAT WAS SUPPOSED TO BE A FEW HOOKUPS THAT TURNED
into pretend boyfriends I thought would last a few weeks
has morphed into months, and there's no end in sight.

Dash is the person I text when I wake up and the man
I call as I'm falling asleep. He's the one I talk to about
Father, and my studies, and how on earth I'm going to be
able to continue with my frat duties senior year as everything else ramps up.

We go on dates to the drive-in and on-campus festi-
vals, party our nights away at my house, and fall asleep in
each other's beds more often than not.

Dash has quickly become my person, and even though

I've always known I'm going to have to give him up, I've hit the point where I don't know how.

"They've got some folk music playing in the quad tonight," he says from the pillow beside mine, playing Snake on his phone.

"Sounds good."

Dash's snake dies, and he tosses the phone aside, rolling over to fling his leg over mine. "We can do something more low-key though. I know you got all funny when we saw Lizzie out the other night."

I shake my head. "That wasn't because of you. We haven't spoken at all since we kind of broke up."

"How do you kind of break up?"

"Well, we were never officially together, so I assume that you can't officially break up in that case. But we ended things."

He nods, fingers trailing over my chest. A look crosses his face that I've seen a few times lately, and it always leads to a conversation I'm not interested in having if I don't cut him off in time.

"What are your plans for summer break?" I ask.

Dash shrugs. "Head home for a bit. I've got some internship applications that I'm waiting to hear back from."

I swallow against the question I know I shouldn't ask. It comes out anyway. "Can I see you?"

"See me?"

"Yeah. Like, we can visit each other. Or meet up

somewhere. Maybe take a private boat out into the middle of the ocean where no one is around but us."

"And what would you tell your dad?"

"Shh …" I slap my hand over his mouth. "We pretend he doesn't exist, remember?"

Dash gives me sad eyes as I remove my hand. "Pretending only lasts for so long."

"It lasts for as long as I want it to last."

His gaze drops, thumb brushing my nipple, before he shakes his head. "Summer sounds like a good time to have a little break from each other."

"A … break?"

"I'm not saying we won't keep seeing each other until then or even when we're back, but … maybe having some distance from this thing will do us both good."

"Why?" I shift out from under him and throw my legs off the side of the bed. "Want to fuck a bunch of other guys?"

He laughs, and it makes my anger burn deeper. This jealousy when it comes to him has never backed off. I've never been able to move on from it, no matter how many times I remind myself that Dash might feel like mine, but he isn't. He never will be.

He wraps his arms around my waist and presses a kiss to my bare shoulder. "I've willingly tied myself to you for half a year now. If I was interested in having sex with other people, I never would have done that."

"Right."

"I'm … attached to you, Arch. It's not healthy. We both know how this ends."

"Maybe I don't want it to end. Ever."

"That's not your call, and we both know it."

I frown, letting those words sink in. How the hell can I have my life apparently made when I don't even get to choose who the hell I share that damn life with?

"If it was …"

"If what was?"

"If it was my choice, and I chose you—"

Dash shoves away from me. "I'm tired of your hypotheticals. Fucking hell, Levine, at some point, we can't keep ignoring the real world. At some point, we have to take a step out of fantasy land."

"Fuck the real world."

"Yeah, well, you can hate on it all you like, it isn't going anywhere." He rubs his hands over his face and shifts so he's sitting beside me. "Unfortunately, neither am I. The thought of you not being here makes me sick. I hate how much I like you. Some days, I think I need you. I *can't* need you. It'll break me."

"Then I guess we're both doomed to be broken."

He takes my hand, but neither of us says a word. It's not like we can argue. It's true. We only did this to ourselves. My heart is going to end up in a million shattered pieces.

So will Dash's.

Because of me.

"Maybe you're right," I whisper. "Maybe we should use summer to take a break." Even saying the words is painful.

He scratches at the black marker he's used to color in his fingernails. "Yeah. It'd make things easier."

"And when we're back?"

"Why don't we decide when we're back?"

In other words, he's hoping to be over me before then. This wave of panic hits me, but there's nothing I can do. I won't fight for us. Father will never accept me with him, so … it's too damn bad.

I hope he gets over me.

I'll never get over him.

"But the break doesn't start before then," I tell him. "I'm going to live in denial until I board the plane for New York."

"Solid plan."

"Unless I drag you on there with me."

Dash laughs, but he doesn't know I'm serious. All it would take was the smallest bit of courage. A rare moment of stubbornness, of wanting, and I'd break. I'd tie Dash to my damn plane, then take him home and introduce him as the man I've fallen for. Even in my imagination, it doesn't go well.

"Hungry?" he asks.

"I could eat."

"Let's head to the dining hall before class."

I agree because I won't eat otherwise and follow him

from the room. We walk side by side, not touching, and every step makes me more and more frustrated. With Father, with the world, but mostly with myself.

The way I feel about Dash isn't going away. It's getting stronger and driving me out of my damn mind. You'd think those kinds of feelings would be enough, that it'd make me draw a line in the sand and grow a fucking backbone.

But no matter how deeply I care for him, my father is still my father. He's still the man who controls my life, my future, and he's still homophobic as hell. The only way for us to have a future is to walk away from him, but there are no guarantees when it comes to Dash. He couldn't even answer me when I asked if we were a real possibility.

Not that I can blame him. He's given me everything I've asked for, and I guess trying to picture us as a real couple was asking for one thing too many.

I can't help it though. Can't stop picturing and wanting. Dash makes me feel more alive than any money or travel or exclusive party ever did, and I don't understand how everything can feel like it's meant to be when I'm with him. We're doomed. But why doesn't it feel like we are?

Every boost, every spark, every flicker of hope that hits me when we're together makes me want to be a better, braver man.

Pity it'll never happen.

15

Dash

TIME HAS HIT FAST-FORWARD ON JUNIOR YEAR, BUT WHEN my lips are on Archie's lips, everything slows. I'm anchored to the moment. Reality doesn't exist, and he gets his wish of us living in a fantasy land. Nothing can touch us here.

He whines, and I laugh into his mouth, gripping the waistband of his pants as I hold him hostage in our place hidden in the stacks.

"I have class," he reminds me.

"Like fuck do I care."

He kisses along my jaw, and the fact he's still so hungry for me has my head spinning. "Maybe if I flunk out and don't become the high-powered lawyer Father wants me to be, he'll be so disappointed the gay thing won't even register with him."

"Good luck with that. You'd just be hitting his weak spots double."

"Are you sure you won't come home with me?" His tone has taken on a desperate edge that is becoming more prominent the closer we get to summer.

"Positive. There is nothing that could get me on a plane to come face-to-face with your dad."

"Not even a blow job?"

"Considering you know how much I love those, my answer still being no should tell you something."

He releases me, a loud sigh escaping his lips as he drags both hands through his chaotic curls. "Maybe I could … not go home."

"Uh-huh."

"I'll run away with you instead."

"Sure thing."

We've had this conversation a million and one times, and I know better than to believe it. I'll humor him, but my patience for pretend is growing thin. What started as surface-level attraction has dug deeper than I ever wanted it to, and now the need to be near Archie is suffocating. I hate that we're about to have a break from each other, know that I'm going to be miserable not texting him every time I think of him, but I need this.

"Am I allowed to say I'm going to miss you?" he whispers.

While we've both made it clear we're not happy about the distance and that our feelings are growing deeper than pretend, it's the first time one of us has openly mentioned the giant wall between us.

I swallow thickly, pressing my head to his shoulder so I don't have to look at him. "No."

"But—"

"I said you're not allowed to say it."

"Dash …"

Panic is ringing in my ears. "Shut up, Archie. There's no point."

"Maybe I want you to know."

"Well, maybe I'm growing sick of your maybes."

Instead of getting offended like usual, his big hands hold my neck. He's learning. Can anger be a love language? I swear when I'm angry at him is when I'm feeling the most.

"I'll forgive you. I'll understand," he says, a slight croak to his words. "If we come back here next year and you've moved on, I … I'll get it."

"Good." I press harder into him. "It'd be the best outcome."

"That's a goddamn lie, but I'll let you believe it."

"*Stop.*" He's getting too reckless with trying to drag our pretend world over into the real one. They have to stay separate. They have to.

Archie's thumb rubs circles behind my ear. I want to melt into him and forget all of the rules, but even though I'm stupidly falling for the man, I'm still trying—not well, but *trying*—to protect my heart in all of this.

His lips skim my ear. "Even when this is over, you'll forever be the greatest part of me."

Stupid, angry tears prick at my eyes, and I refuse to let him see them. Refuse to acknowledge that when it comes to breaking me down, he's won. He's played me and made this all so much more complicated than it ever needed to be, all because he wanted to catch feelings.

Maybe I didn't.

Maybe I never wanted to feel this way. But Levine was determined to make it happen, and now look at me. Fucking close to *crying* over a man who was never mine.

"Oh my—oh my *god*."

I tense at the female voice, eyes shooting wide.

"Lizzie?" Archie croaks.

"What … what …"

My heart is in my throat, strangling me as I whirl on her. "It isn't what it looks like!" Which might be the dumbest response I've ever had because everyone knows that when you say that, it's *exactly* what it looks like.

"You mean you two weren't *cuddling* in the stacks?"

"No—"

"We were."

My focus flies to Archie instead. "Don't."

"Don't tell me what to do!" It's the first time ever he's

actually raised his voice at me. His soft face is a hard mask as he glares down Lizzie. "We're together. I'm gay. Now that you know, what are you planning to do about it?"

Her mouth opens and closes a few times. "I … I don't know."

"Then let me make it simple for you." His pained, tortured voice I'm so used to is gone, and *this* Archie is someone I can believe grew up with a silver spoon up his ass. "You've always wanted to be a Levine: consider it done. Keep this secret to yourself, and the second we graduate, I'll put the biggest, shiniest ring on your finger that your friends and family have ever seen. I'll be a dedicated husband—" The first crack in his voice makes me want to comfort him, even as the words he's saying are tearing me in two. "—and you'll have everything you've ever wanted in life. All I need is one year. One year to be who I really am before I become the person everyone else wants me to be."

"But … you're gay," she whispers.

"I've always been gay. You've never been able to tell before."

"Archie, I …"

"Do we have a deal?"

Lizzie's eyes flick to mine, and she quickly redirects them to the floor. "I … umm … okay. Yes. I guess … fine. Yes."

"Good." It feels like all the air leaves the library. Sweat is prickling along my hairline, and no matter how much I force my lungs to try and work, it isn't getting any easier.

"I'll just … go …" Her voice is soft as she all but runs from us.

Archie turns and yanks me into his arms, all the pretend control evaporating as he falls against me. "Fuck. *Fuck.*"

I can't hug him back. I know I need to. I know he's hurting and probably scared, but my heart won't slow down, and my thoughts are impossible to catch hold of. This is how it was always going to go. Him marrying a woman was always going to happen—he knew it, I knew it—but apparently, I didn't *know* it. Not like this. Not like looking her in the eyes and knowing she'll share a house with him one day. She'll get married and probably have his babies and—

I'm stiff as I pull back out of his arms.

"Dash?" Confusion floods his eyes. "What's wrong?"

"What's … what's wrong?" I almost laugh, but I might be closer to a panic attack than anything else. "What's wrong? Everything is fucking wrong."

"I don't understand."

My mouth falls open. "You … do you know what just happened? You proposed to her."

He shakes his head. "It was more like … a deal."

"A *deal*?"

"To make her keep our secret."

I might throw up. Those stupid tears are back, and I'll do anything to try to stop them from spilling over. "I can't do this."

His body goes rigid. "What do you mean?"

I stare at the place Lizzie disappeared to. "I can't …" The hurt curls around my chest, and it hits me, for the first time, that trying to protect my heart was the real pretend. "Shit. I think I'm in love with you."

Happiness takes over Archie's face, and he closes the distance between us, trying to hug me even as I hold him back. "I love you too. I've never felt like this before. Never thought I ever would." His hand cups my jaw and forces my head up, making me meet his hopeful eyes. "You kill me, Dash. Every day, I fall for you more. Every day, I think things could never get better than they are right now, and every day, you prove me wrong. I love you so much." He tries to kiss me, but I turn my head, shrugging out of his hold. I hate that he said all that to me. Hate that after everything I saw, the reality that just smashed through our bubble, that he's giving me the whole truth.

I fucking hate it.

"I thought I told you to shut up."

"What do you mean?"

"How could you say that? How could you tell me all that after you've agreed—sorry, made a *deal*—to marry someone else?"

"You know why I did that."

I do. I'm an idiot. It's not Archie's fault; it's mine. All this time, I've been trying to protect him and put him first, but I forgot to look after myself in the process. "I do." I take a deep breath. "So I hope you know why I have to do this."

His face falls. "Do what?" He knows though. I can read every expression on his handsome face.

"Don't make me say it."

"I'm going to make you fucking say it. You want to end it, then you're going to have to say the words."

I want to land one on his chin, even though I know my anger is more directed at me than him. "Fine. You want to hear it? It's over, Levine. Just like it was always going to be."

Maybe he thought I was bluffing because tears immediately spill onto his cheeks. "Don't. Please, you can't."

"I have to."

"You can't tell me you love me and then end things!"

I wish I'd never said that word. "I can and I am. I can't be the reason you ruin your life. It's not fair."

"Dammit, Dash, I don't care."

"*I* do. It's not fair *to me*. My heart feels like it's tearing in half."

Archie sniffs and scrubs his hands over both cheeks, turning them red, but not the red that I love. "Okay." He can barely get the word out. "That's what you want."

The unhinged laugh that's been threatening this whole

conversation finally comes. "When has this ever been about what I want?"

I storm away from him, half hoping that he'll chase me and refuse. Tell me he's never letting me go. Every step that separates us drives the pain deeper. I'm fucking crying before I even get to the library doors.

16

Archie

"IT'S SO NICE TO HAVE THE WHOLE FAMILY HOME AT ONE time," Father says, clapping me on the shoulder and squeezing harder than I'd like. My teeth clench a little tighter against the need to say something. "Especially when they bring such lovely friends with them."

Lizzie smiles up at him from her place beside me at the table, and I feel sick. The servers hurry to bring the food out once Father is seated, and talk immediately turns to business. My older brother is a solicitor and firmly under Father's thumb.

"Senior year, Archibald," Father says suddenly.

I jump from my vacant thoughts. "Ah, yes."

"I hope you'll be knuckling down and applying yourself."

"Always."

"And that you're not spending too much time with—" He waves a hand toward Lizzie. "—pretty girls."

I catch myself from laughing. "Never do."

"Trust me," Lizzie adds. "That's not a problem."

"Excellent." Father nods toward Mother. "Did you get it?"

She grins, and my heart stops as she pulls out a ring box. "Picked it up this morning."

"Ah, what's—what's that?"

"Grandmother's ring."

This cannot be happening. My head swims so forcefully I almost pass out on the table. "Why do you have it?"

"To make sure it fits," my mother says, like I should already know the answer. And I don't know, maybe I should. Maybe I should have been prepared for the train wreck my life was about to veer toward, but every single thing since Lizzie caught me in the library with Dash has taken me by surprise. My heart squeezes thinking about him. Almost my entire two weeks of break have been spent trying to figure out how to get him back.

"Here." Mother nudges the ring box against my elbow. I stiffly reach for it. The dark velvet brushes my fingertips, nowhere near as soft as Dash's hair.

"Ah …" I go to hand the box to Lizzie when Albert stops me.

"Hold on, now. You should be the one to put it on her. Where's your romantic side?"

Up your fucking ass, Albert.

Lizzie audibly inhales before turning to face me. Her smile is dazzling, but there's something off about it. Not what I'm used to from her.

"You okay?" I murmur.

"Let's just do this," she mutters back through her teeth.

I crack the box, and a diamond the size of my thumbnail twinkles back at me. That nausea hits me again, and I'm sure I sway this time, vision swimming to the point the diamond multiplies.

"Would you give us a moment?" Lizzie asks, plucking the box from my fingertips and setting it on the table. She pulls me from my chair, and I don't bother to fight her, just go limp like the noodles in the middle of the table.

She closes the door softly behind us once we step out into the hall.

"Struggling, huh?" she asks softly.

"What do you mean?"

Lizzie pulls her long hair over her shoulder, twisting the strands around her fingers. "I'm nervous too."

"You are?"

The look she gives me is downright patronizing. "You think I want to tie myself to a … to a man like you?"

I'm dumbfounded. "You don't?"

"Of course I don't." She scowls. "Seriously? You think I don't want some kind of epic love story? I'm twenty, for Christ's sake."

"Then why did you agree to our … to our deal?"

She waves her hands around like she can't find the words. "You're a *Levine*. My parents would shoot me and bury me in the yard if I said no to you."

I slump against the wall, letting the weight of everything sink in. Lizzie, Dash, me. All suffering because I won't come out of the closet. Am I the biggest asshole ever?

"No." She leans next to me.

"No what?"

"You asked if you were an asshole. You're not. Well, *most* of the time."

"I didn't realize that was out loud."

We're quiet for a moment, and Lizzie glances back toward the dining room.

"*He's* the asshole," she whispers. "It's not fair that you have to hide."

"Yeah, well, in case you hadn't noticed, Father isn't all that interested in fair."

"If you told him about … you know. At least there'd be a reason I could give my parents for turning you down. Even they wouldn't want me married to … surely."

"Right."

"I won't tell anyone though."

That hits me deeper than I'm expecting it to. I glance up and try to show my relief, even though I feel so fucking dead inside. "Thank you."

"So. Now that's all out there, I guess we have a ring to try on."

"I guess so."

"Unless—"

"I can't."

She sighs. "That's the shitty part in all of this. You can. I've seen it. You know how to command a room. You have your trust. You're not reliant on him anymore, and in just over a year, you'll be well on your way to becoming a kick-ass lawyer. I've known you for a few years now, Archie, and I know that you're capable of anything."

"But he'll—"

"What? Turn his back on his own son? Do you really think that? You have nothing to lose. He does. Your dad might be a strict asshole, but he loves you."

"He won't love this."

"Of course not. He'll probably be a real dick about it. But which sounds worse? Being married to me forever and never seeing your boyfriend again or having your dad be pissed off at you for a while. I'm not trying to diminish it, because it *will* be hard at first. But one of those options sounds like it will be hard forever."

Hard forever or hard for right now?

I know Lizzie has an agenda. I know she's invested in my coming out, but considering no one, ever, comes into that area of the library and she did? Lizzie, who needs me to give her a reason to get out? Is this some kind of god-given nudge for me to get my act together while I have someone in my corner to support me?

I hunch forward, holding my knees. "I can't do it."

The door beside us cracks open, and I don't have the energy to stand. To keep on pretending.

"Archibald, what's going on? Are you ill?"

Father's voice sends a chill down my spine.

"Maybe a stomach flu," Lizzie answers for me.

I glance up, head heavy. "I'm not sick." I am. I feel like I'm about to empty my stomach.

"Then what's going on? You're keeping us waiting."

I can feel Lizzie's curiosity burning the side of my face.

"I'm not coming back in there."

"Why?"

"Because I can't do it. I can't marry Lizzie." Every word is terrifying. So hard to say, but the more I let out, the more that keeps coming.

Father's jaw tightens. "Go back inside," he tells Lizzie.

"I'm very sorry, Mr. Levine, but I can't."

"This is a family matter."

"Actually, this affects me more than you." She takes my hand. "I'm going to stay."

I grip tight to her hold.

"What's going on?" Father demands. "I don't like being kept in the dark."

"Give me a fucking second."

"Excuse me?" He straightens to his full height. "You will speak to me with respect."

"Respectfully, I'm getting there. I just need a moment." My eyes fall closed, and I try to picture Dash's face. His smiles and the way his hands look against my skin. His bright eyes and messy hair. My heart feels too big. Too much. I never want to lose this feeling.

And when I open my eyes again and look at Father, all I see is an aging man. Someone stern and blunt who is holding on to control because he knows he's losing it.

Do I choose to be miserable for him?

Or do I choose myself? And Dash? And all the happiness he brings me?

I stand from where I'm slumped against the wall, surprised I'm as tall as he is. "I'm not going to marry anyone."

"You will do as you're told."

"Unless you tell me to marry my boyfriend and somehow change the law so it can happen, then I can't imagine we'll be seeing eye to eye on that point."

He blinks at me, face frozen as he processes my words. "Your ..." His eyebrows rise. "*Boyfriend*?"

"Yes. His name is Dash Lewis, he's the prettiest man I've ever seen, and if it's up to me, I'm going to keep him forever."

"Lewis. Boyfriend." Father looks like he's stroking out.

"Should I grab you a chair, Mr. Levine?" Lizzie asks, and he stares at her like he's never seen her before.

"A chair?"

"You look in shock."

His teeth gnash, and he turns on me. "You will end things. Now. I will not allow my child to be seen as a boy-loving pansy. I won't have it!"

Rage burns in my gut. "It's not your choice."

"So long as you live under my roof, it is!"

"Then I suppose I'll be packing my things."

"What's all this shouting?" Mom asks, stepping into the hall and quickly closing the door after her. "Lizzie, darling, go inside."

"I'll stay with Archie, thank you."

"Please tell me no one is pregnant." Her voice goes faint.

"Unless the male body has changed recently, I don't envision that being a problem."

She frowns. "I'm s-sorry, what?"

"I'm gay, Mother. And Father has decided that means I'm no longer welcome here."

She turns to Father with wild eyes. "You can't be serious."

"Of course I am." His cheeks are splotching red. "I gave him the option to give up these ideas—"

"It's not an option," Lizzie cuts in, but he ignores her.

"I won't have it here. I won't—"

"He's our *son*."

"I didn't raise this."

"I don't care. I don't want him to go." My mother turns to me. "Archie, honey, you're staying with us. We're your family."

"Family support each other," I point out.

"I won't support this!" Father shouts.

"Then I'll leave. I don't care anymore."

"You'll care when you're cut off."

"My trust is more than enough to keep me going."

"Take a breath," Mother snaps. Her voice is louder than I've ever heard it. "You don't approve, we understand, but think of the alternative. Think of what happens when people find out you've thrown your own son out onto the streets."

He snorts. "The Empire hotel is hardly the streets."

"Others won't see it that way. People are becoming more sympathetic to that … lifestyle. Do you want others to talk?"

"The second they find out about him, he's all people will be talking about. What will it do to his brother?"

"Free up more women for him to sleep with, I'd imagine," I snap. I'm done with this. Done with them talking about me like I'm not here. Mother might not want me to go, but even if she changes Father's mind, I won't be welcome.

So I'll go where I *am* wanted. Hopefully. Dash didn't

want me to get outed because of him, but now that it's happened, will that be enough? He said he loved me—that can't be a lie. He's not the type of guy to fuck around with people's feelings like that, and if I don't have to hide now … could we do this for real? No more pretend boyfriends, just us?

I ache for that.

Before either of my parents stop arguing, I leave. I jog upstairs, pack a bag, and book a flight.

Praying the whole time that Dash still wants me too.

17

Dash

ARCHIE:

I need ur address.

I look at the text message for a long time, wondering whether I should respond. We agreed to a clean break, no contact, but *daaamn* I want to write back to him. I'm burning with curiosity over why he needs my address. It's been the longest two weeks to ever exist, and *this* is the message I get out of the blue.

Does he want to send me something? A thrill shoots through me over the most likely outcome. Unless it's some kind of restraining order, wanting my address has to mean gifts, right? What would someone like Archie think to send someone like me? I'm insanely curious to see if it's something dumb and stupidly expensive that I'd hate or if he actually knows me. Would he put thought into it? What would he come up with?

I tug at my hair and glare at my phone screen, restless with my lack of a decision.

We agreed to a *clean break*. I want to say it's been good for me, but it hasn't. I've moped around the house and been snappy with everyone. The only time I'm not thinking about him is when I'm busting my ass at this stupid internship.

I can't even escape him in my sleep.

You know what, screw it. Maybe this can be my test for him.

If his gift is something he thinks will impress me because of the price tag, he's not the guy for me.

If it's something he actually puts thought into … well, then I'm fucked.

Before I can talk myself out of it, I reply with my address.

It's torture not to keep checking my phone all day, but either Archie is regretting asking, or he's gone back to respecting the whole no-contact thing. Either way, I don't hear from him, and apparently, it doesn't matter how moodily I stare at my phone, it doesn't change things.

"Dash, honey, visitor!"

I groan as Mom's voice filters up to me. A few of my high school friends are still in the area, but I'm way too irritable to be company today. Mom couldn't have made up an excuse for me, could she?

I sigh, not bothering to change out of my stale shirt, and leave my room, hoping I look sick enough to be able to beg off hanging out today.

Only when I thunder down the stairs and glimpse who's at the door, I suddenly wish I could have a redo of the last three minutes of my life.

"Archie?"

His smile makes my heart stop. "Umm, hey. I probably should have called first, but I didn't give myself time to stop and think about the details."

Yep, I'm fucked.

Sure, it probably cost a lot of money for him to be here, but the fact I get Archie, in real life, and not some stupid gift is doing things to my heart I didn't think was possible.

I launch myself into his arms. "You idiot. What are you doing here?"

His arms wrap around my waist, and his nose buries into that spot between my neck and my shoulder. My gut soars at the contact, and it's painful to have to anchor it back to earth again.

"I needed to see you."

I pull away from him. "Do I need to explain a break to you again?"

He glances around and then leans in. "Is there somewhere we can talk?"

"Yeah, of course." I take his hand and pull him inside, pushing the front door closed behind us, and then lead the way upstairs.

"Your house is cute."

"Shut up."

"I'm being serious."

"I know you are. That's why I said to shut up." We reach my bedroom, and I shove him inside, then can't stop myself from grabbing him and tugging him into a kiss. "You shouldn't be here."

Archie cups my face, smiling bigger than I've ever seen him. "I had to see you."

"Again … break."

He shakes his head roughly. "I don't want to be on a break. I don't want to break from you ever again."

"Arch—"

"I told my dad."

"What?"

He lets out a nervous laugh. "Lizzie was there, and they were pressuring me with a ring, and then she said she didn't want to marry me either but can't say no because of who my family is. And I thought about you and how if I let this end without giving it a real shot, I'm going to be miserable for the rest of my life. You're the kind of guy I'll hunt down in the phonebook in twenty years' time and call just to hear him breathe. Probably find out where you work so I can walk by, hoping to catch a glimpse of you. I'll dream about you and daydream about you and regret, every day for the rest of my life, that I didn't at least try. I love you, Dash. I wasn't lying about that. And I realized I can live and be happy if my father walks away from me. I can't live and be happy without you."

My jaw is opening uselessly as I stare at him, trying to process and let the words sink in. "You told him?"

His eyes crinkle the way I love. "That's what you got from all that?"

"It's a pretty big bomb to drop on a guy and expect him to be paying attention afterward." Still, the rest of his words sink into my consciousness. He still loves me. He wants to try. "So, if you've told your dad …"

"I have no reason to hide anymore. I mean, obviously, we still need to be careful, and I won't be shouting it all over campus, but there are gay couples at our school. I've seen them. We could be one of them."

I throw myself at him, kissing him so deeply I never want to let go. My heart is full for Archie, for me too. The level of bravery he would have had to show to tell his dad is more than I'd ever have in a lifetime. If he wants to try, I'll try right alongside him. Archie Levine isn't the kind of guy you give up in a hurry.

"I am so proud of you," I tell him.

"Does that mean we can put an end to the breakup?"

It's the lightest I've ever felt in my life. "Immediately. Let's pretend it never happened. I … I still can't believe this. How did he take it?"

"Horribly."

"I'm sorry."

"I'm not." He shrugs. "He can't claim to love me if it's only on his terms. You love me on mine, and you always have. Even breaking up, you did that for me—I've never had anyone put me first. Not like you. Whether we make it to forever or not, I'll never regret telling him. I'll never regret you."

I walk him backward until he lands on my bed. "We're gonna make it to forever, Levine. You have a jealous streak, and I kinda like to win. We'll do it. I know we will."

His hands find my hips, and he grins up at me as I drag a hand through his curls. "You're telling me I'm the only man who'll ever get to touch you again?"

"The only one." Feeling wicked, I add, "Unless you're into sharing."

His face twists, and he lets out a huff like an angry bull. "I will never share you."

"What about my dick?"

His fingers tighten.

"My ass?"

His jaw clenches.

"My mouth, then."

Archie grabs me and flips me so I'm under him on the bed. "You're mine. Your dick, your ass, your mouth. Last time, we were pretending, but this is for real. I want you. All of you. I'm not pretending anymore."

"Good." I cup his face. "I like this reality so much better."

We spend a few minutes making out while I try to wrap my head around this being it for us. We've agreed to forever. I'm prepared to put in the work. My heart has never felt so full and right. I rut my hardening dick against his leg.

"Nope." He climbs off me, even as I try to pull him back down. "I haven't met your mother yet. We're not having sex under her roof."

"Ah. So, you want to look her in the eye before you fuck her son. Got it."

He groans and pulls me to my feet. "And there you go guaranteeing I can never have sex with you under her roof, ever."

"I hope you have money for lots of seedy hotel rooms."

"Without Daddy's money, I'll be tight for a while, but I will always, always give you what you need."

I light up, but before I can say "orgasm," he cuts me off.

"And no, you don't need to come right now. You need to introduce me to your mother as your boyfriend. Then we need to make plans."

"So he really cut you off, then?"

"I have no idea, but I'm not going to wait around for him to."

"We have a spare room."

He looks vulnerable as he brushes my hair back. "You think your mother would mind?"

"Okay, no more 'mother.' It's Judy. You'll make her feel old. And she's basically the coolest mom you'll meet. She'd let you stay in my room if I asked."

"We're not going to ask that."

I sigh. "Fine. But only because you've had a long day. Tomorrow is another story."

"Tomorrow." Archie lets out a long exhale. "I like the sound of that."

"Tomorrow. Next week. Next year. Always. I'm going to give it all to you."

Like every bit of tension he's ever held melts out of him, Archie folds his body into mine. I mean every goddamn word too.

Archie Levine is the only future I want.

18

Dash

I'D LOVE TO SAY SENIOR YEAR IS A BREEZE, BUT NO. IT'S a fucked-up mess of homophobic frat boys, guys trying to hit on my man, and intrusive questions about how I turned Archibald Levine the Third gay.

I've never been so happy to reach graduation or so proud that Archie had to go and beat out my "cum laude" with a "summa cum laude." As far as I'm concerned, both those titles contain the word *cum*, and that's one of the best memories of our relationship.

Did I call him the cum lord for the rest of the day? Yes, I did. Did he prove my point that night? Many, many times.

I haul the last of our boxes into a New York City apartment, borderline terrified that this city is going to bankrupt me. Sure, this place was always earmarked for Archie and law school, but I was never supposed to be part of that equation. The fact his dad still sent him the keys to move in has me suspicious, but I'm not too proud to say no to a free space in New York. Especially with a view like this.

"That's your worried face," Archie says from where he's unpacking the kitchen with way more dinner settings than we have friends.

I gently kick the side of the box with a *thunk thunk thunk* as I worry over whether to bring it up. We've never held back with each other before though, so I'm not about to start now.

"What if your dad says he doesn't want me living here? You didn't tell him I'd be moving in with you, and let's face it, if he kicks me out, I can't afford a place in New York. I'll have to move back home and—"

Archie approaches, hands finding my upper arms, where he gives me a reassuring squeeze. "Where you go, I go. Simple as that."

"But—"

"No." He pulls me closer, and it's easy to be confident when he is. "We struggled through school. We've had a hard start to our life together, but that's not going to be a common theme here. All it comes down to is the simple fact that I love you. If Father tries to be high-handed, he'll be down one lawyer son, and I'll have no regrets about walking away from it all. My life doesn't mean anything without you."

"Anyone ever told you that you're kinda intense?"

He laughs and presses his forehead to mine. "You. Daily."

"Good. Just testing your mental state. It passed, so I'm going to hold you to that. If your dad kicks us out, we'll be on the street together."

"I have too much money for that to ever happen, but we'll definitely be putting New York behind us. Until then ..." He turns me in his arms to look out at the skyscrapers around us. "Welcome to your new life, Dash Lewis."

I wrap my arms tighter over where his are holding me. "I know we'll never be able to get married, but what ... have you ever thought about kids?"

"I have many thoughts about children."

"Well, would you want one?"

He's quiet for a moment. "With you?"

I almost roll my eyes. "Obviously, you can't impregnate me—and thank fuck for that with how obsessed you are with filling me with your cum—but like, there are options, aren't there?"

"Are there?"

"Well, adopting. Or fostering. Surrogacy."

He does that quiet thing again. "You want that?"

"Only if you do. I'm in this. We're forever. That's

never going to change for me, and adding a kid to our lives sounds amazing."

"And once it's here, who would look after it?"

"Either of us." I turn away from the view to look at the most incredible man I've ever known. His eyes are more blue today because of the watery cloud cover outside. "It could take forever for us to make it happen, but if it happens early and you're in law school, I will. If it's later and you have good benefits, then you can. The logistics are the unimportant part. If you want one is the important part."

"Would you be happy with me if my answer was no?"

"Of course. You're my everything, but …" My lips hitch with the image of a little Archie running around. "I think it would be an amazing bonus."

"Yes."

"Really?" I don't even try to hide my disbelief.

"Why is that surprising to you?"

"Because you're a controlling neat freak? Because you like schedules for your life and no schedules for our sex life. A kid would mess all that up."

"I …" Something changes behind his eyes. "I want that as soon as possible."

"You're sure?"

His small laugh buoys me. "No. I'm not sure. I'm terrified, but we're doing it anyway. Because whenever I do things scared is when the best things happen."

"You're a romantic one, Levine."

"And you're still a scoundrel. Tempting me into everything I didn't know I could hope for."

"I'll make it my aim to terrify you for the rest of our lives."

Archie's forehead kisses mine. "It's terrifying enough to know you won't even have to try."

EPILOGUE

Archie

Twenty-one years later

I'VE NEVER BEEN AS AT WAR WITH MY EMOTIONS AS I AM right now. I've always known this moment was coming, always known it was for the best, but it doesn't mean I'm any happier about us being here.

I'd thought we had more time.

"Stop, Dad," Charles says, blinking back the same tears I am.

"I can't help it. You were supposed to stay our baby."

Dash wraps a comforting arm around my waist. "What he means to say is that we're proud of you, and we'll always be here for anything."

Our son smiles and pulls us both into a hug. Campus is full around us, and I'm glad Charles was never one of those kids embarrassed over hugging his parents. God, it just makes this harder.

If he'd picked a New York school, he could have stayed at home with us, and while West Haven U isn't far, it's far enough that he can't commute there and back every day.

I squeeze him tighter for a moment before I have to let him go.

"You're gonna have the best time," Dash tells him. "College is meant for fun, flirting, and friends. Remember that."

"But not at the expense of your degree," I hurry to add, making Dash smirk at me.

"Yes, yes, education is important, but that isn't the part you need reminding about."

Charles is patient as he says, "I'm rushing Kappa. I'll be fine."

"*Kappa?*"

The three of us turn toward the voice. A guy, clearly a freshman and carrying a huge duffel bag, pauses by us.

"You're not rushing Rho Kappa Tau, are you?"

Charles shifts. "Ah, yeah?"

"Ooooh, we're going to be rivals. Sigma Beta Psi, baby."

My son laughs and holds out his hand. "Charles. Maybe we can try not to hate each other too much."

"I can't make that promise." But the guy shakes Charles's hand anyway. "Zeke."

"Nice to meet you."

They let go after a painfully long handshake, and this punk backs up a step, then two. His lips hitch upward on one side as his eyes sweep over Charles in a way that has my alarm bells ringing. "I guess I'll see you around."

He leaves, and my son's face is a whole lot redder than it was before. Fuck me. I barely want him moving on campus, let alone *dating*.

"You've got everything?" Dash asks, completely oblivious to our son being fully grown.

"Sure do." He glances over his shoulder toward the dorm. "I should probably go."

I pull him into another hug before he can stop me. "College is going to be amazing."

"I know." He's smiling when he pulls back. "Everything will be fine. Relax."

Then our son grabs his bag, sends a quick wave our way, and hurries off.

I'm watching long after he leaves.

"Are you going to start crying on me?" Dash asks.

"Not sure yet."

"We knew this was coming, and Charles is a smart kid. We got super lucky with him."

"We did. He's the best."

Dash wraps his arm around me again and props his chin on my shoulder. It's been amazing to see the progress for queer people over the years, and the reality that we can stand here like this and no one looks twice is the most freeing kind of relief.

Charles will never have to worry about keeping himself hidden.

Speaking of …

"Did you see the way that … *Zach* kid looked at Charles?"

"What do you mean?" The amusement in his tone tells me he knows exactly what I mean.

"You saw it."

"The blatant checkout and how our son went red as a tomato."

I scowl. "Sometimes I wish he'd inherited your genes. The blushing is the worst."

"I dunno." Dash drags a finger down my cheek. "It's a fun game to see how red I can make you go."

I cringe. "I don't want to think about that becoming a fun game for our son."

He roars with laughter. "It's college. I remember exactly what I was doing at college, and let me tell you, he's going to have his fun."

Not able to shake the melancholy, I turn to my

husband. "It feels like it all went so fast. One minute, he was a baby, and now he's here."

"I'd never give up being a father for anything, but you have to admit it'll be nice to just be us again. We only had a few years together before having him."

"I'm going to miss him."

"So will I. Badly. But I'm happy for him getting to lead his own life now."

I take Dash's hand, and we start our walk back to the car.

"Remember the first time we ever talked?" he asks. "You hunted me down in a hallway in a jealous rage."

"There was no jealous rage."

"In my memories, you came in, beating your chest, then threw me over your shoulder and carried me back to your sex dungeon."

I sigh, used to my husband's ridiculous antics and loving that part of him has never changed. "What happened next?"

"You had your filthy way with me and then chained me to your bed. Wouldn't let me go for weeks, and when you finally did, you got all possessive and shit. Understandable—my ass is gold." He lifts his left hand, gold band catching the sun. "Now, somehow, I'm locked up for good. A complete sex slave to my heathen husband."

I slap my hand over his mouth. "Dear god, stop talking."

"Ah, but there's that blush I love so much."

And like that, he's completely distracted me from my sadness at saying goodbye to Charles. I hope this part never changes: the way Dash is so playful and loving. How he always knows what I need.

We had a rocky few years with my father, but after Mom died, he came crawling back into our lives. Some days, I think he's trying to relive our relationship through Charles. It doesn't bother me much anymore, but I am glad our son gets to have that relationship with his family.

Even if I missed out.

And through it all, I've done everything I can to lighten my son's pressure and hope he never has to live his life for someone else the way I did.

Dash was always the fun parent, and seeing him with Charles only made me love him more.

I tug him to a stop. "Thank you."

"You're welcome." He cocks his head. "But why?"

"There was a lot of bullshit when we started out. Then there was a lot of bullshit after I came out. Then when we had Charles. And still, things aren't always easy. But you've supported me every single step of the way."

I get one of his rare, soft smiles. "How could I not? Before I even knew you, I knew you were special. We fought for our life together because we knew it was worth it."

Dash is worth every fight. Always. For the first time

ever, I feel positive about a new stage of our life beginning.

Because Dash has proved he'll be there for it all.

And I'll love him just as completely through everything.

AUTHOR'S NOTE

Thanks so much for reading these gorgeous guys!

The fact you keep showing up for me, release after release, means the absolute world! My dream has always been to have a career as an author and it's mind-blowing to me that I get to live it.

If you're a lover of signed paperbacks, special editions, audiobooks or merch, don't forget to check out my store.

You can find it through the link or QR code: www.saxonjamesauthor.com

OTHER BOOKS BY SAXON JAMES

ACCIDENTAL LOVE SERIES:

The Husband Hoax

Not Dating Material

The Revenge Agenda

FRAT WARS SERIES:

Frat Wars: King of Thieves

Frat Wars: Master of Mayhem

Frat Wars: Presidential Chaos

DIVORCED MEN'S CLUB SERIES:

Roommate Arrangement

Platonic Rulebook

Budding Attraction

Employing Patience

System Overload

NEVER JUST FRIENDS SERIES:

Just Friends

Fake Friends

Getting Friendly

Friendly Fire

Bonus Short: Friends with Benefits

RECKLESS LOVE SERIES:

Denial

Risky

Tempting

CU HOCKEY SERIES WITH EDEN FINLEY:

Power Plays & Straight A's

Face Offs & Cheap Shots

Goal Lines & First Times

Line Mates & Study Dates

Puck Drills & Quick Thrills

PUCKBOYS SERIES WITH EDEN FINLEY:

Egotistical Puckboy

Irresponsible Puckboy

Shameless Puckboy

Foolish Puckboy

Clueless Puckboy

STAND ALONES WITH EDEN FINLEY:

Up in Flames

FRANKLIN U SERIES (VARIOUS AUTHORS):

The Dating Disaster

And if you're after something a little sweeter, don't forget my YA pen name

S. M. James.

These books are chock full of adorable, flawed characters with big hearts.

https://geni.us/smjames

WANT MORE FROM ME?

Follow Saxon James on any of the platforms below.
www.saxonjamesauthor.com
www.facebook.com/thesaxonjames/
www.amazon.com/Saxon-James/e/B082TP7BR7
www.bookbub.com/profile/saxon-james
www.instagram.com/saxonjameswrites/

www.ingramcontent.com/pod-product-compliance
Ingram Content Group UK Ltd.
Pitfield, Milton Keynes, MK11 3LW, UK
UKHW040858240225
455493UK00001B/66

9 781922 741547